UNCOFFIN'D CLAY

Gladys Mitchell

UNCOFFIN'D CLAY

St. Martin's Press
New York

Library of Congress Cataloging in Publication Data

Mitchell, Gladys, 1901–
  Uncoffin'd clay.

    I. Title. II. Title: Uncoffin'd clay.
PR6025.I832U5   1982   823'.912   82-5586
ISBN 0-312-82857-8   AACR2

First published in Great Britain by Michael Joseph Ltd.

For CHARLES and PATRICIA
with thanks and love

Beaminster, Melplash, Mapperton, Hooke
And Toller Porcorum; none named in this book.
For I have changed a vital fact or two,
So this tall story never could be true

Contents

CHAPTER 1

A LOOK AROUND
THE NEIGHBOURHOOD

It all began last Spring while I was staying with my brother
Innes and his wife at the house they had bought in a little
town called Strode Hillary. They had bought it when Innes
retired from his editorial post to become a freelance writer,
and Mary had given up her singing so that they could spend
more time together than had been possible while both were
working. Mary had been often away from home when her
concerts took her to distant counties or abroad, and she had
confessed to me that she was quite prepared to abandon a
career on the concert platform and 'dwindle into a wife' as
soon as Innes was free.

They were a lively, hospitable couple – Innes distinguished-
looking, witty and apt at quotation, a lavish host and
extremely sociable; Mary a poised and beautiful woman,
ash-blonde, blue-eyed, serene and very charming. They had
lots of friends, and I thought it was good of them to invite a
widower brother to stay with them and occupy the guest-room
to the exclusion of people they might have preferred. The
atmosphere was always civilised and harmonious in their
company, and I had always enjoyed my visits to their previous
home.

This was the first time I had seen the new house. It was
modern and convenient and I was looking forward to a
leisurely and pleasant week. However, this visit turned out to
be vastly different from anything I had expected and it
began – now I look back on events – to show its altered
character on the very first morning of my stay.

I had arrived in time for dinner on the previous evening. On
holiday I am usually an early riser and the next morning, I
remember, I had bathed, dressed and shaved by the time
Mary called out from their bedroom, 'Tea's up, Michael!' I

had known her for so long that I was always invited into their
room for the early cup and looked forward to this introduction
to the day, for there was vicarious romance in sitting on a bed
at the feet of a lovely woman, even though her husband was
present. (Not that I grudged Innes his good fortune. My own
marriage had been a happy one and my feeling for Mary was
almost entirely brotherly, although I was aware that Innes
kept his eye on me. This flattered me unduly and made me feel
younger and happier than I usually did, so, far from objecting
to it, I took his watchfulness as a compliment.)

As for Mary, she had no brother of her own, so I merely
filled a family gap so far as she was concerned. I understood
this, and kept myself well within bounds. I cherished my visits
to her and Innes, and had no mind to risk their being
terminated by any lapse of good taste on my part.

I accepted a cup of tea, mutely pledged her with it and,
when she had gone off to take her bath, I said to Innes, as I got
up and strolled towards the window: 'Well, how are you going
to like it here?'

'Very much,' he replied, getting out of bed and joining me.
'The house is what we wanted, the people round and about are
kind and we get invitations from everywhere and give our own
little parties, of course. There's a very good music society
which we have joined, I am getting bits of work to do for my
old journal just to keep my hand in and myself out of mischief,
and Mary – bless her heart! – is as happy as Larry. Things
couldn't be better!'

'Famous last words!' I said. He laughed.

'Be that as it may, look at the garden and the view!'

My own bedroom window in his house looked over the
pleasant enough aspect of a wide square which made a
turning-point for cars in a cul-de-sac which terminated at the
closed end with a fenced bank, and at the open end in a quiet
road which veered left towards the town. The view at which I
was looking was wider and very different. I gazed appreciat-
ively out over the countryside and promised myself some
early-morning walks.

Some miles away – I did not know how far – there rose a
conical, tree-clad hill. Against it, and appearing to dwarf it

because the distance between them was so great, was the golden-grey, pinnacled tower of the parish church.

House-tops in the high street of the quiet old town cut off the base of the tower from my view, but, between the jumble of roofs and that part of Innes's garden which was directly below the window, stretched a long green paddock and to the right of the paddock rose an equally grassy hill. This was crowned by a row of dark, sparsely planted trees below which was a well-kept hedge. The effect, I thought, was that of a mildly beneficent god with his hair on end and a necklace of jade around his neck.

This reminded me of a gift I had picked up in New Bond Street when I had accepted Mary's invitation.

'I've brought her a present,' I said, half-turning away from the window.

'Have you? How kind,' he said. 'How do you like the garden? We had it landscaped.' Immediately below the window there was a broad stone terrace from which there descended one fairly steep and one shallow step to a partly paved sunken garden. The paving enclosed a considerable rose-bed, not, of course, yet in flower, and outside the paved portion were broad borders of spring flowers backed by plants and shrubs already in bud.

On the terrace itself were two enormous tubs of teak which had been brought from the delightful cottage which Innes and Mary had had near Tring. The tubs, as I had always seen them at that time of year, were filled with what, to me, was the tumultuous glory of the April daffodils, flowers which, for some reason, always reminded me of Mary herself, although 'tumultuous' was hardly a word which expressed what I knew of her.

A hedge separated the garden from the paddock, and at one end of it was a slightly leaning, grey-boled walnut tree, too old now to bear fruit, but of gracious symmetry, and neighbouring it were two close-leaved, dark-green cypress trees. At the other end of the hedge, but not in the garden itself, swayed a sapling ash as graceful as a young silver birch tree.

Nearer the house, on the opposite side of the garden and behind the border plants, there was a bush of myrtle, sacred to

Venus, and the tree beneath which Phaedra had waited for Hippolotos, exerciser of horses. While Phaedra had waited, I remembered, she had pierced the myrtle leaves to while away the time, and the prickings can be seen on every leaf to this day. So much for legend which can always explain the otherwise incomprehensible.

My thoughts carried me further. In ancient Israel the Hebrews believed that by eating myrtle leaves they could detect the presence of witches. I mentioned this to Dame Beatrice when, later on, we met. She greeted the remark with an eldritch cackle of laughter and remarked that she numbered a notorious witch among her ancestors, a statement I had no difficulty in believing. I added, I remember, that there was a Gentile, if not exactly a Christian, belief that by crushing the myrtle leaves in the closed palm of the hand it was possible to test the faithfulness of the marriage partner. If the leaves crackled, divorce was probably the best solution. I did not mention murder, but another of those disquieting cackles indicated that, as my friend Michele Slung would say, Dame Beatrice even then had crime on her mind.

Mary, looking rosy and smelling delicious, came back into the bedroom.

'Out you go,' she said to me. I retired obediently, went downstairs and picked up the morning paper from the front-door mat. I am an avid reader of newspapers when I am at home, but on holiday I cannot be bothered with them, so, after settling myself on the long couch which was sideways-on to the french windows, I scanned the headlines on the front page and then put the paper down and picked up the parish magazine which was lying beside me.

It was an impressive little booklet, I thought. On its crimson cover, apart from the price (which argued some wealthy subscribers at ten pence a copy), was a heavy black cross on a shaded circle. Around the whole device were the names of the five rural parishes which were served by the vicar of Strode Hillary. Prominent among these and placed at the top, was Strode Hillary itself, where I was staying, and around the arms and stem of the cross were the other four: Aries St. Peter, Paulet Marquise, Lower Gushbrook and Courtleigh Purton, names, I assumed, of historical or topographical significance. Aries St. Peter was an intriguing juxtaposition of the secular and the sacred, Paulet Marquise incredibly aristocratic and Courtleigh Purton reminiscent of some stately home, possibly of Tudor origin. None except the purely descriptive Lower Gushbrook suggested John Betjeman's: 'Gloved the hands that hold the hymnbook, Which this morning milked the cow,' so I felt that Lower Gushbrook and I might have something in common. Little did I guess what that might be, or I might have packed my bags there and then and made what P.G.W. calls 'the quick dash for life'.

I had questions to ask at breakfast.

'We don't know the origin of the names,' said Mary. 'We've only been here a matter of months. If Michael is interested, Innes, why don't we take a run in the car this morning and let him see something of the countryside?'

'Why *five* parishes?' I enquired. 'Are they very close together?'

'No, quite widely scattered and some are not all that easy to reach. This town, Strode Hillary, used to have a vicar all to itself, and I suppose the other parishes had theirs, so either this lumping them all together under one incumbent is an economy measure, or else there aren't enough vicars to go round, one would think,' said Mary.

'Or not enough churchgoers to warrant five livings,' said Innes. 'Would you like a cross-country trip, Mike?'

'I see they're going to beat the bounds,' I said. 'There's a sketch map in the parish magazine.'

'Well, we can follow the same route, if you're interested. You'll still be here at the time they do it, so we can show you the lay-out. We can even join in the doings if you like. It's a church thing – blessing the sowing of the crops, and all that – so it's being carried out on Sunday, beginning at Ropewalk, and then going to one of the farms to the south and finishing at Aries St. Peter, at the vicarage there.'

'That's a very strange name,' I said, as we started out. 'What on earth has the first sign of the zodiac to do with the keys of heaven?'

'You'll know when we get to the church,' said Mary. We

had set off at half-past ten, proposing to have a ploughman's lunch at a pub and our cooked meal when we got home. Mary did most of her own cooking and, over the years, I had learned to look forward to her dinners, although, in the ordinary course of events, my appetite is capricious owing to the heavy-handed efforts of various 'obliging' domestic workers to sustain me since my wife's death.

'Come to think of it,' said Innes, who was driving, 'As we can't very well call at the farms which will be, largely, the object of next Sunday's exercise, we won't be able to follow the actual route today, so we'll just make it a sight-seeing tour, taking in the villages as we come to them. First we'll have a general view.'

We turned away from the church and the houses and were immediately in open country. A road tunnel through a hill and a turning off to the right brought us to a wide area where was a famous viewpoint. Below us was the little town we had just left. Around were the hills and over them an April sky flecked with wind-blown clouds. Innes, aided by an Ordnance map, pointed out the approximate locations of the other four parishes.

'We've never been to Aries St. Peter or Lower Gushbrook,' he said, 'so I hope I'll be able to find them.'

'But if you haven't been there, how did Mary know that I'd realise, when I saw it, why the village is called Aries St. Peter?'

'It's in all the guide books,' said Mary, from her seat in the rear, for they had insisted upon giving me the seat next the driver. We had to return to the town to begin the pilgrimage proper, and as we drove along the high street and past the market square, I realised, as I had not done on my drive through it in the darkness of the previous night, what a delightful old town Strode Hillary was.

There were houses of all periods – the lath and plaster of Tudor times; tall, narrow, dignified Georgians; a double-fronted coaching inn with a royally-collared stag as its sign; old-fashioned shops around the market square which had its butter-cross and its horse-trough; almshouses now restored to make a parish hall; a beautiful house – Queen Anne, I thought – set back from the road behind lawns and flower-beds;

intriguing narrow streets opening off the main street and one of them leading to the church; and there was even a little river which entered the town unobtrusively at the eastern end and was soon lost to sight as it meandered out south-westwards away from the houses.

We took a right-hand bend out of Strode Hillary and almost immediately were in a countryside of hills and deep green valleys. The nearest of the parishes was Paulet Marquise. We pulled up opposite the church and got out of the car. From the roadside I gazed in frank disbelief at the edifice confronting us.

'It isn't real,' I said.

'According to the guide books, it's a copy of the church which was first built here,' Mary said. 'Do you want to take a closer look at it?'

I am a devotee of church architecture and this was something quite out of the ordinary. It was a far too perfect copy of the earliest type of Norman church – squat, square tower, round-headed windows and doorways with chevron moulding around the arches, an apsed end – but it also had transepts and, on an outside wall, more chevron moulding where no Norman mason would have dreamed of putting it, since it served no purpose except that of incongruity.

Although the outside might have deceived an inexpert eye, the inside was so unorthodox that even a visitor unused to churchgoing must have been astonished. The altar, instead of being at the east end of the church where the apse was, had been placed at the end of the north transept and the apsed end was now a baptistry, complete with a late Victorian marble font on three stone steps.

The crossing and the south transept now formed the nave of the church and held the pews for the congregation. What had been the original nave was curtained off. There was nobody except ourselves in the church, so I went over and pulled the curtain slightly to one side. To my further astonishment this disclosed what was most obviously the parish hall. There was a platform at the west end for lectures or the performance of simple plays; a gymnastic box and horse and four balancing forms were at one end of the stage and a useful-looking cupboard stood in the opposite corner. A stack of chairs, of the kind which sit so conveniently on top of one another in order to conserve space, completed the furnishings.

'Ah,' said Innes, joining me at my peep-hole, 'economical and admirable, don't you think? When they beat the bounds there is going to be a tea-and-bun fight in here. If we join the revels we may be able to snatch a cuppa. Mary attends church once a month and also entertains the vicar at our house when he's on visiting rounds, and she is doing a weekly stint in the school dinnerhour instructing the female adolescents in make-up and polite society manners, so I should think we'd be eligible.'

'Do the local magnates join in the jamboree?'

'Oh, sure to, for the look of the thing, you know. This is still hunting, churchgoing, magistrates' bench, anti-poaching country – not that there isn't a certain amount of bad blood between some of the notables. There are people you can't invite to meet each other at cocktail or dinner parties, and there's the local sheikh – not that *he'll* be joining in Sunday's procession, being, one supposes, a Moslem of rigid views.'

'A sheikh?'

'No less. He lives at Bourne Farley, the Paines' old place.'

'What's his name?'

'I believe he's got a string of names, like Royalty. I call him Abdul the Bulbul Ameer, after the student song, you know.' He began to sing, a thing I myself would never have dared to do with a trained professional like Mary standing by.

' "The sons of the Prophet are hardy and bold," ' chanted Innes, ' "And quite unaccustomed to fear, But of all the most reckless of life or of limb, Was Abdul the Bulbul Ameer." '

'*Is* he reckless of life and limb?' I asked.

'He must be. Nobody hereabouts wants him either as an acquaintance or a landlord. There's a lot of bad feeling around and about. He has had a number of the local lads up before the Bench for trespass and wilful damage and in every case some anonymous well-wisher has paid their fines for them and kept them out of chokey, which was the alternative to their coughing up the money. No, Abdul ain't loved. In fact, I sometimes suspect the Chairman of the Bench, old Lord

Maumbury, of putting up the money for the fines himself, not that he can afford it. He's got one of these interminable lawsuits on his hands to try to settle the ownership of a local property called Fell Hall. The house itself can be written off as a dead loss because they had a disastrous fire there and the place is gutted, I believe, but there's a chance of selling the rest of the estate for building plots, and that could be worth a fortune with land the price it is, not to mention the rumour that there's oil in these 'ere parts. They've started drilling in some stretches of the county already.'

'Under the sheikh's auspices?'

'Oh, I don't think so. All his business interests are in the Middle East, but he has bought what is said to be the remains of one of King John's hunting lodges, later converted into a Tudor mansion. The Paine family was crippled by death duties and forced to sell. I'm told he took over the house and estate at a fabulous price and keeps a harem there of beautiful *houris*. He goes about with a bodyguard, but I don't suppose they are armed.'

'He sounds a colourful character. Have you met him?'

'No, but I don't believe the stories about the harem and his servants' reputed attempts to procure the local girls to add to his collection. However, the *hoi polloi* loves horror stories, especially when they border on the indelicate. As for the local nobs, well, I suppose they'll accept him in the end, if only because of his money, but at present he's a *parvenu* and a foreigner and there's enough of the old prejudice left in most people for the persistence of a belief that "the wogs begin at Calais". Thank goodness Mary and I live in nice, comfortable, middle-class anonymity and don't have to take part in the local boycotting and skulduggery. Mind you, I don't approve of wealthy Arabs taking over lovely old places such as the Paines' house, but perhaps that's better than letting them fall into complete decay. At least these fellows have the money to keep them up.'

Well, nothing is gained by some kinds of argument, so I made no comment. We returned to the car and went on to Courtleigh Purton.

'The Sunday procession – all cars, of course, because of the distances between the parishes – will be calling at one of the farms near here,' said Innes. 'We can have a look at the church, if you like, but the showpiece is, of course, the manor house.'

We left the car in the road and walked down a long, broad avenue of beech trees with, planted between the trees, clumps of daffodils. There was a right of way through the park, but the house itself was in private ownership and not open to the public. Even so, the glimpse we had of it was well worth the visit. There was a gracious, beautiful, seventeenth-century frontage in golden stone. The house had slightly projecting wings, the entrance was protected by very fine wrought-iron gates, the gate-piers were crowned with stone eagles and were recessed with round-headed niches, purposeless but charming. It was a most delightful place.

'Does this house figure in Sunday's revels?' I enquired.

'No,' replied Innes, 'I'm told the family are away. The procession will go past the church and on to one of the farms from here.'

'Is the church interesting? You did mention it.'

'Not particularly interesting, and the village perished at the time of the Great Plague.'

'This isn't the manor house your sheikh bought?'

'Good Lord, no! These owners would never sell.'

After Courtleigh Purton we found a pub for our lunch, and after lunch we lost our way. This, Innes assured Mary and me, was not because of the cider which had accompanied our bread and cheese, but because he was not yet familiar with the countryside and so was dependent upon signposts. These proved either to be conspicuous only by their absence or, where they did exist, unhelpful and even misleading.

We pursued Lower Gushbrook and Aries St. Peter along lanes only just wide enough to take the car, past farms, fields and hedges, between high banks reminiscent of South Cornwall, up and down winding hills, past open country and through woods, past ash trees, oaks and, occasionally, pines, along a high, seemingly interminable ridge from which we could see across the landscape for miles and, here and there, we even obtained a glimpse of the sea.

Once or twice we pulled over to let an approaching farm
tractor get by, and on another occasion Innes stopped the car
almost in a ditch to allow an immaculately clad rider on a
high-mettled horse to pass us. We received a courteous gesture
of thanks and I asked who the rider was.

'Goodness knows. I don't hunt,' said Innes.

'How do you know that *he* does?'

'With a horse like that? Besides, they all hunt around here,
the farmers, too – although my neighbour tells me there have
been some rows about gates left open and young crops
trampled. Of course the real locals wouldn't offend like that,
but, unfortunately, some of the big estates have been bought
up by people who have made their money but don't – and
never will – really "belong" in the countryside.'

'Your sheikh, for example?'

'I shouldn't think he hunts. He owns a racing-stable
somewhere, and an enormous yacht, and plays golf and used
to play polo. If it weren't for local feeling about his buying the
Paines' house and so – in the local view – dispossessing one of
the oldest families in the county, he might even be popular. I
believe he gives enormous sums to charity and has rebuilt the
village hall. They ought to be grateful to him, but they ain't.'

On we went, past a small, exquisite gem of a Tudor house,
past a fruit farm and then, on a long downhill track, past
stables, a paddock, a large cottage set on a grassy slope and
then past another farm which had a dairy herd of Jerseys. It
was after we had crossed a bridge over a narrow stream and
come at last upon another signpost that Mary said:

'I hate to spoil the fun, but if you two are expecting to get
any dinner tonight, I think we'd better take the hint from that
signpost and go to Fylditch. The car knows its way home from
there. I'll invite Martha Lorne to pop in for a cocktail and
then I can ask her the way to Aries and Gushbrook so that we
can go there tomorrow.'

At dinner that night I gave her the present I had brought
with me. It was a necklace with matching earrings, a charming
set. The earrings were in the form of tiny marguerites with
dark-blue translucent centres, and the necklace, on a very fine
silver chain, was similar – except that the marguerites varied

in size from one which was only a little larger than the earrings, to one which was twice their size. The necklace terminated in a flower-bud made of diamonds.

I saw Innes widen his eyes when Mary opened the case and took up the necklace. She was delighted with it.

'You shouldn't have,' she said, and kissed me. 'But I'm glad you did. Is this why you asked me to wear blue tonight?'

'No. I like you in blue,' I said. When she had gone up to bed that night and we were having our last drink, Innes said,

'Ought that stuff to be insured, Mike?'

'Insured? Lord, no, I shouldn't think so,' I said. 'It's quite pretty, but it isn't all that special.'

'Diamonds?'

'Oh, well … '

'Where did you get it?'

I named the shop and he whistled.

'Well,' I said defensively, 'I miss not having a woman of my own to buy frippery for.'

'If it's all the same to you, I shall get it valued for insurance,' he said. 'You're an ass, Mike!' But as he said it he leaned forward and gave me a brotherly smack on the thigh. 'She's thrilled with it. I expect she's got it all on and is sitting at the dressing-table mirror admiring its reflected glory.' Then he added, 'I suppose it came out of your last book, did it?'

'No. I had a bit of luck with the gee-gees,' I said. 'Backed a rank outsider and it came home at thirty-three to one.'

'What was it called?'

'Oofy Prosser.'

'Ah,' he said, 'I'd have backed it myself if I'd known that.' We were both Wodehouse fans. He came upstairs behind me, laughing so heartily that Mary called out from the bedroom,

'Is it a rude joke, or can anyone join in?'

'Not innocent young women like you,' he called back; and I knew that, because the money had come from a lucky bet and not by the sweat of my brow, plus the equally lucky name of the horse, any doubts as to the suitability of my having given Mary an expensive toy had been removed from his mind. I was glad. I was very fond of him in a casual, brotherly way, and we had always had an excellent relationship.

CHAPTER 2

LOWER GUSHBROOK AND
ARIES ST. PETER

Mary's conference with Martha Lorne, whom I had met over cocktails, must have achieved results, for, having lazed away the following morning and had an early lunch, we found Aries St. Peter and Lower Gushbrook without difficulty. I had come down on the Sunday evening, and this Tuesday the weather had become boisterous – for we were not far from the Channel – and somewhat chilly, so we were well wrapped up in the car, which was unnecessary while the heater was on, but essential when we got out and were assaulted by the wind.

Mary was driving, Innes beside her, and I was on the back seat and slower at seeing the signposts than he was. I was not much concerned with following our route. My lunch had settled nicely and I was content to sit and watch the banks and fields and hedgerows go by.

Violets and primroses were out, there were still some hazel catkins where the hedges had not been ruthlessly cut back, and here and there were willows. I recognised *salix caprea,* the Great Sallow, which produces its catkins in time for Easter – early, as it happened, that year, for the children were already back at school. Unlike some of its kind, this willow is not dependent on streams for its existence, for it grows in woods and tall hedgerows. I thought of my wife, Imogen, who had loved what she called pussy-willows, and I was only recalled to the present when Mary said,

'I knew we were right when we passed the turning to that last farm. We ought to be able to see the church tower of Aries St. Peter soon. Martha says the church stands on a little hill.'

'There was an argument going on in that last turning,' said Innes. 'Looked pretty heated, too. Unusual, in these parts. They're an easy-going lot around here. Ah, there's the church on our left.'

Although we could see the church, it still took us a little time to reach it, and the lane we were on turned so much that sometimes the church appeared on our right, sometimes on our left, and sometimes almost straight ahead. Our lane mounted gradually but steadily, now between banks of dead bracken as the land rose on either side of us, and higher up the hillside we passed ash and beech trees and, crowning the steep rise, there was a ridge of pines. A baby deer ran across the road when it heard the sound of the car, and Innes remarked that we were passing one of the largest estates in the county.

Soon we were among silver birches and more pine trees. A little further on, Mary pulled up where the lane widened as it became part of the village, and on our left, perched above us on its eminence, was the church.

A flight of wooden steps with a helpful handrail led upwards to a path through the churchyard, and there before us was the church itself, surprisingly large (as village churches so often are), with a fifteenth-century tower, a thirteenth-century chancel and fourteenth-century windows to the nave.

The interior held only one striking object. This was the font, and I understood at once how the village had received its name. The font was just inside the west doorway of the church and was well lighted by the windows, which were of clear glass with no colouring. The font had been formed from the capital of a Roman pillar and part of its shaft. The rubble had been hollowed out a little in order to accommodate the basin to hold the baptismal water, and the capital itself was carved with enormous spirals reminiscent of the curling horns of a ram, and at the angle of the cushion capital was a ram's head.

'Amazing,' I said, studying it. 'A mixture of the sacred and the profane. Whatever induced them—?'

'I know,' said Mary. 'Some people even think that the base formed part of a Roman altar, but that has been ruled out, I believe. We thought you'd like to see it today, as the church will be crowded on Sunday before the vicar gives his celebration supper to those who've been beating the bounds. The font is unique, I'm sure.'

There was nothing else of interest in the church. In fact, so well lighted and so otherwise dull, with its late nineteenth-century south arcade and aisle and its pitch-pine pews and darkly-cemented walls, was it, that the splendid views of the countryside from its exterior, when we went outside again, were almost a necessary compensation for the drabness (except for that astonishing font) within.

'Lower Gushbrook lies over there,' said Mary, pointing. 'I don't know why we're going there, except that the procession passes through it. There's nothing much about it in the guidebooks.'

Lower Gushbrook, however, was a very pleasant surprise to us. As Mary, guided by Mrs Lorne's knowledge of the countryside, had told us, the village was on our way home. It was a straggling little place with some ugly buildings and a few picturesque houses and cottages. The church, nineteenth-century and unremarkable, was not worth the visit we paid it. The village, however, had two remarkable and, to my mind, beautiful features, although in the light of what happened later, I doubt whether I am justified in using such an adjective as 'beautiful'. All the same, Lower Gushbrook became of so much importance to ourselves, the police, the national press and Dame Beatrice herself, that I feel it merits description.

So far as I remember, we came upon its stretch of water suddenly. We had turned a corner by a jumble of cottages which were apart from the rest of the village – this, we discovered, was further on – and there on our left was this stretch of water too large to be called a pond, nor sufficiently vast to merit the title of lake, but which might justifiably be given the poetic appellation of a mere. On our side the bank was flat and grassy. The opposite shore was wooded, with a hill rising behind it. We discovered later that the woods were on an island and that the mere itself had a further grassy side beneath the hill.

There was a swan on our side, and there were mallard on the water, a brownish speckled duck and a brightly plumaged drake with feathers of green on his head, a white collar and a purple breast.

At the roadside, but running between the grasses, was the stream from which the village took its name. Although, so close to its source in the surrounding hills, it was, indeed, little

more than a brook, it flowed fast and cleanly, a lovely little
chalk-stream dashing and splashing along over the bright
pebbles in its bed, with here and there some cresses and other
water plants which occasionally interrupted its rapid flow.

We got out of the car to look at it, for there is magic in
running water, and this little stream, bubbling, gurgling and
singing, was delightful. After a bit, I strolled back along its
bank to look over at the ·mere. While I was standing there,
Innes came up. He thought he had better get back to the car,
he said, in case it had to be moved to let another vehicle pass,
but Mary joined me on the broad grassy verge and we stood
side by side looking over the water.

'Isn't it beautiful here?' she said. 'I'm glad we came.' By
what seemed to be mutual reaction, we strolled on. Beyond the
turn of the road which had brought us in view of the mere, a
lane branched off, following the course of the brook, and led to
some cottages, but where road and lane came together, some
boys (presumably) had built a miniature clapper bridge across
the stream.

We crossed it and found a well-trodden path which seemed
to lead to the narrow end of the mere. We followed it and so
found out that the woods I had supposed to be covering the
further shore were on a long, narrow island, but to this there
was no access except by wading.

'I should think the village kids have a wonderful time here,'
I said. 'Nothing beats grass and water and woods.' We turned
and walked back towards the clapper bridge on our return to
the car, but stopped to look at a half-submerged duck-punt
which was lying in shallow water at the head of the mere.

The woodwork was rotting away and the boat was half-
filled with a mixture of soil and leaf-mould in which some
tufted sedge and young osiers were growing. Around the punt
I could see the submerged stems and skeleton-like rigid, thin
dark leaves of the water-crowsfoot, although so early in the
year there were no flowers.

Mary joined me.

'I wonder whose punt it was, and how long it's been there,'
she said.

'Probably used at one time to cut waterweed,' I said. 'It

wouldn't have been used for pleasure-boating in a place like this. Does the procession come along this road?'

'I don't know. Anyway, this is one of the five parishes. I suppose they will stop at the church before going on to the trout farm and then they'll finish up at Aries St. Peter. That will be the last stopping-place. There will be a church service there, followed by cider and something to eat at the vicarage, and then everybody who has seen the whole thing through to the end will meander home, I suppose.'

'Is the procession a time-honoured thing? Does it date back a long way?'

'Oh, no. I daresay there was something of the sort in the Middle Ages – you know, blessing the crops and so forth – but not on this sort of scale. The route will cover more than forty miles, I should think, by the time all the farms have been visited. This "five parishes" business is quite an innovation. They did it last year, Martha Lorne tells me, but before that, if there ever had been a tradition of blessing the crops, it had fallen into limbo so far as Strode Hillary is concerned. After all, we aren't a farming community in Strode Hillary. We're professional or business people, for the most part, town-dwellers, anyway, by nature, whether retired or not. The nearest farm must be quite a way outside our town.'

I looked down again at the waterlogged punt and remarked that water-meadows were one of the features which would have to be part of heaven if I were to enjoy myself there.

'You're sure you're going there, then?' said Mary, laughing and taking my arm.

'I've never forgotten the spotted snakesheads – *fritillaria meleagris* to you – in the Iffley meadows when I was a child,' I said, 'and the kingcups and yellow iris along the Stour and the Frome when I fished here in Dorset, and the ragged robin with its attendant swallow-tail butterflies on the Broads, and the purple loose-strife and meadowsweet and watermint by the Itchen.'

'So what plants are these growing in the punt? I had no idea you were a botanist,' said Mary.

'I'm not, but all fishermen notice water-plants and become, in spite of themselves, amateur naturalists. The plants in this conservancy of the punt, reading from left to right, are the tufted sedge, two up-and-coming osier willows, the bog-bean, whose roots were once used to make flour, the marsh cinquefoil (I think), the water bistort and the arrowhead. The flowers of the arrowhead are unisexual, thus pre-dating modern trends by goodness knows how many centuries.'

' "Oh, no man knows, Through what wild centuries roves back the rose," ' said Mary.

'Don't steal Innes's thunder,' I said. She released my arm and we stepped out briskly and joined him in the car.

'Mike has been giving me a botany lesson,' she said; and then, irrelevantly: 'I wonder who lives in those houses overlooking the far end of the lake? They don't look like villagers' cottages, do they?' (There were three of them about fifty yards further on.)

'Probably bought up and done up by retired Londoners,' said Innes. 'It goes on all the time and there's a lot of feeling about it in some quarters. People cruise around in their cars, find a remote spot with a view, especially if there's a stream front or back of the property or it's near the sea or a lake, and snap it up, no matter how decrepit it is. Then they spend a lot of money on repairs and decoration and other amenities – not worrying if there's cesspool drainage and no damp-course – and settle down to live happily ever after. In these days of motor cars it doesn't matter how far you have to go to find a house and then do the kind of shopping to which you've become accustomed. Those would be the sort of people who would live in these three houses.'

'One of them is up for sale,' said Mary. 'How about it, Mike?'

'Yes, if I didn't have to live in London,' I said. The drive home was along narrow lanes, sometimes between high banks which, after the manner of railway cuttings, hid everything but themselves from view, sometimes through woods where the trees arched into a tunnel over the road, sometimes into open country with a view over miles of hills, valleys and sky. I thought nostalgically of that mere-side house for sale, and sighed.

We were invited to have drinks that evening with Martha

Lorne. I had gathered already that she was one of those women who seem to collect all the local news by telepathy, but perhaps it came to her via the Women's Institute, of which, it appeared, she was a prominent member. This time she was primed with information of an unusual and startling kind.

'Somebody has taken a pot-shot at the sheikh,' she said, 'and from behind his own trees, too.'

'Thus adding insult to injury,' said Innes. *'Was* he injured?'

'No. He was with Mr Winters and the shot went through Winters's hat.'

'What was Winters doing at Bourne Farley?' asked Mary.

'The sheikh wants to buy Long Fallow to round out his stud farm,' Martha replied.

'But Long Fallow belongs to Farmer Breedy, I thought.'

'I know. The sheikh wants Winters to negotiate with Breedy, I suppose,' said Martha. 'If anybody can push the deal through, Winters can, and then Mr Okeford will see to the conveyancing, or whatever solicitors do.'

'It will need more than a smart negotiator to talk Amos Breedy into selling,' said Innes. 'He's a tough customer, I hear.'

'Oh, well, I don't know about that. *Money* talks, and the sheikh can afford to buy anything he wants, however fancy the price,' argued the hostess.

'What do *you* know about Farmer Breedy?' Mary asked her husband.

'Nothing much,' Innes answered, 'but a couple of chaps were talking in the shop when I went in to pay for the papers on Saturday morning, and the story came up then about the sheikh wanting to buy Long Fallow. These fellows were saying that the town and country planning lot would never let the sale go through. Long Fallow is agricultural land. It will never be leased merely as extra ground on which to exercise horses.'

'Perhaps Winters will plead that the sheikh wants to put it under oats to *feed* the horses,' said Martha. 'Did you find Aries St. Peter and Lower Gushbrook quite easily?'

It was such an obvious change of subject that I was somewhat surprised.

'Thanks to your briefing of Mary, who insisted, most

sensibly, upon taking the wheel, yes, we did,' I said. 'Are you joining the procession on Sunday, Mrs Lorne?'

'I don't know yet. It all depends upon whether I get a lift. It is visiting a number of farms and there will be hymns and prayers and blessings at each one. I hate repetition. It's so boring, so perhaps I won't bother.'

'Then you have no use for the repetitive seasons of the year, the accidents we call birth and death, the recurrence of the festivals of Christmas and Easter, your birthday and your annual summer holiday and the punctual payment of pensions and dividends,' said Innes ironically. It was the first indication I had had that he disliked her. She laughed the recital off.

'Oh, that's different,' she said. 'Did you hear about the row at the W. I. meeting?'

'No,' said Mary, as nobody else appeared to be prepared to answer. 'What was it about?'

'Guide dogs for the blind. Mrs Cassett proposed that the dog which was allotted to poor Miss Crippins, who passed away last week, should be mated and the puppies trained to take the mother dog's place.'

'Not a bad idea,' said Innes. 'Given five pups and Mendel's theory, two will be useful, two impossible to train, and one very dangerous.'

'That isn't Mendel's theory,' said Mary.

'I know. It ought to be six pups, not five. Think of the young lady called Starkey.'

'Why should I?' asked Mrs Lorne. 'I've never heard of her.'

'She had an affair with a darkie,' said Innes. 'Fear of the Race Relations people warns me to say no more.'

'Oh, it's a *limerick!*' said Martha. 'One evening we'll have a limericks versus limericks competition at the W. I., the most outrageous to win the jackpot.'

I laughed.

'Your evening would be as blue as the booze-up after the last match of a season of Coarse Rugby, Mrs Lorne,' I said. 'I wouldn't risk it, if I were you.'

'No, indeed,' said Innes. 'Limericks, Martha, are like the poet's story of Deirdre. They are for men and, after them, their sons and their sons' sons. A good dirty limerick is wasted on women.'

'Oh, you and your quotations!' she said. 'Don't you ever say anything unless it's in inverted commas?'

'Who's half-quoting now?' retorted Innes. 'But I can cap it. "Sometimes I say goodbye." It's time we went home.'

'Where does my half-quotation come from? I don't recognise it,' she said, looking pleased with herself nevertheless.

'A.A. Milne, Act One, *Make-Believe*. The princess says, "Don't you ever say anything except good morning?" '

'Oh, I'm a princess, am I?'

'All women are princesses,' said Innes, making her a polite but ironical bow.

'Why don't you like Mrs Lorne?' I asked, as we walked home. Martha's house was in a side street by the little river which flowed past her front garden just before it veered away from the town. As the evening was fine, we had not bothered to get the car out.

'I've a feeling she's a bit of a snooper. She told us that she has keys to most of the houses around here so that she can get in and feed their pets and generally keep an eye on things when people are on holiday, but I wouldn't let Mary give her ours. I've a feeling that, in spite of her helpfulness and general appearance of goodwill, she's a very dangerous person and doesn't even *know* that she is,' he answered. 'I don't suppose the poison ivy knows that it's poisonous, but the fact remains. We didn't really need her help when we moved in, but she's as clever as the tradespeople in spotting newcomers and calling on them. I have a suspicion that Martha Lorne is going to cause a lot of trouble some day.'

'Because she collects information and then gossips about it?'

'I don't know. Still, so far as Mary and I are concerned, there's no information to be collected in the sense that gossip could harm us.'

'Of course it couldn't,' said Mary. 'All the same, I wish we could rid ourselves of Martha. Our other friends don't like her—'

'*I* don't like her,' said Innes.

'But, after all, she's a widow and one doesn't want to be unkind.'

'You're too thoughtful about other people,' I said. 'All the same, from my own point of view, I'm very glad you are.'

'Oh, you're different,' she said. 'We love you, Mike.'

'Speak for yourself – or, rather, don't,' said Innes, 'unless you want to put an end to a feast of brotherly love.'

He spoke lightly, but I knew we were on slightly unsafe ground, so I returned to the subject of Mrs Lorne.

'Why don't you and your friends like Martha?' I asked.

'She isn't our sort, that's all. But, as Mary indicated, she's the sort of clinging burr that it's very difficult to remove. She cottoned on to us almost as soon as we moved in and we don't know how to dislodge her.'

Innes and I helped with the dinner when we got home and at eleven o'clock we sent Mary to bed while we did the washing-up.

'Talking of Martha Lorne,' said Innes.

'Yes?'

'You know what my job was, Mike.'

'Yes, of course.'

'Well, although I was a journalist, not a vet, I had quite a lot to do with animals. They can't talk in our language, but they have a marvellous talent for communicating their emotions and their needs.'

'One communicated with me, I remember, by biting a chunk out of my trousers,' I said, recalling a catch-as-catch-can session with a friend's half-grown but only half-trained and extremely boisterous Alsatian.

'I'm serious, Mike. I developed an extra sense which men (I exclude women) don't normally possess. I can *smell* evil, just as I'm convinced that animals can smell the abattoir long before they get to it.'

I became uneasy. Although our surname, Lockerbie, comes from a place in the Lowlands, Innes and I have Highland blood, and I did not like his air of prophecy. Mary came down in her dressing-gown just as Innes dropped a plate.

'I knew we ought to have left the washing-up until the morning,' she said. 'What are you two hatching?'

'Gunpowder Plot,' I said.

'Do you really think somebody shot at old Bluebeard?' she

asked. Innes answered, as he stooped to pick up the pieces of the plate he had dropped,

'No, I think the shot was meant for Winters. Nobody who shot at the sheikh could possibly miss. There's so much of him. Pity the marksman didn't aim a bit lower. Winters is a nasty job of work. The world would be cleaner without him.'

'But who fired the shot?' I enquired.

'I wouldn't put it past Breedy,' said Innes. 'I wonder when it happened?'

'Not longer ago than this morning, otherwise Martha would have told us before,' said Mary. 'It certainly hadn't happened when I asked her for directions to Lower Gushbrook. She would have been bound to mention it.'

'What about this chap Winters?' I enquired.

'Aged about forty-five and definitely a bad egg. Call him the local con-man and you wouldn't be far wrong,' said Innes. 'He doesn't belong in these parts. Hiding from his London creditors, I wouldn't wonder.'

CHAPTER 3

CRIME WAVE

On the following morning the post brought an urgent plea to Innes to contribute a leading article to his old journal. The editor was ill and the sub-editor felt that Innes was the best man to come to the aid of the party. I knew that Innes's leading articles, always thoughtful and informative and spiced with wit, had been a main feature of the journal, so when, apologetically, he said he was afraid he would have to spend the morning working, I said that I quite understood and would leave him to it. I lifted an eyebrow as I looked at Mary, but she shook her head.

'Sorry, Mike, but I'll be needed to look up his references, I expect. Mrs Platt will be in to do up the place and I'll tell her to cook you some lunch, so you won't go hungry. We shan't bother, except for having a snack.'

'I'll take a walk and get lunch out,' I said. The idea of spending the morning with Mrs Platt and a vacuum cleaner, the noise of which I find almost intolerable, and of having her cook for me alone (a matter I felt sure a sensitive charwoman would regard as victimisation or, in her parlance, a put-upon) had so little appeal that my reaction was automatic.

Mary looked relieved, I thought, so, apart from my own feelings, apparently I had taken a popular decision. As soon as breakfast was over and the washing-up left for Mrs Platt to deal with, Innes and Mary went upstairs to the library and I picked up my ashplant and walked downhill towards the centre of the town.

When I reached the market place I turned down Church Lane, but soon after I had passed the church the road mounted, so instead of climbing the hill I turned on to a footpath which went alongside the little river.

The morning, chilly at that time of year, was fine. I soon

began to enjoy my walk – I have always, even when my wife was alive, been fond of my own company and glad to indulge my own thoughts without the necessity of sharing them or of having them interrupted. The little river, which ran fairly swiftly here, for it was still close to its parent source in the hills, was company enough, and the kind of company which suited me best when I was out in the country.

I met nobody until I came to an unfenced bridge not more than three planks wide, which spanned the river and appeared to offer access to some woods on the other side. Standing in the middle of the bridge and looking down at the water was a swarthy young man wearing good tweeds and a bright yellow polo-necked sweater.

As I could see that there was no room to pass him on the bridge, I said, as a hint to him to move onwards or to come off the bridge on my side:

'Is it all right to take the path through those woods?'

He looked round.

'Who wants to?' he asked.

'I'm out for a stroll,' I said, 'and the footpath on the other side appears to lead into some woods.'

'Spring guns and man-traps,' he said.

'I beg your pardon?'

'You don't want to go in there. They'll kill you.' He looked down at the water again. 'Not really deep enough, do you think?'

'Deep enough for what?'

'Drowning yourself.'

'I've no idea,' I said, 'but if you wouldn't mind letting me pass ... '

'Oh, that! Sorry.' He came off the bridge on my side. I raised my hand in acknowledgment and crossed over. When I looked back before I entered the woods, he was on the bridge again, staring down at the water.

My woodland path soon began to climb. The dead leaves underfoot were thickly-fallen and damp. The trees were mostly oaks, but as the path mounted the oaks thinned out and gave place to hazels. Near the top of the rise it was bare except for coarse grass, and when I reached the summit of the ridge I

could see below me a large house and, in the far distance, the
squat tower of a church.

Coming towards me was a man with a gun and a dog, a
rough-coated retriever. I wondered whether I was trespassing,
but he gave me a perfectly civil, although perfunctory,
'Good-day' and, with a word to his dog, passed me and went
downhill and into the woods which I had left behind me.

I stood still and looked about me. It was fresh and breezy in
the upland air, but my climb to the ridge had warmed me and
I was not averse to standing and gazing and feeling the wind
in my face. Now that I was able to give it full attention, I
could make out that the house I had seen was not much more
than a shell. I wished I had brought my binoculars, but they
have something in common with my camera in that they are
never to hand when they are most needed.

From where I stood the downward track was a lot steeper
than the path by which I had mounted, and my calf-muscles
were beginning to resent their duty of acting as brakes by the
time I reached the bottom of the hill. The path swung to the
left, for the forward track was barred off by a wired-up wicket
gate, reinforced by two posts much higher than the little
gate itself and also strung with wire, two or three strands of
which were barbed. Beyond the gate a path led into more
woods.

However, there was nothing to prevent my following the
path to the left. It broadened out and ran between hedges and,
about half a mile further on, one of the hedges was broken by
wide entrance gates and, to the side of them, there was a
cottage which obviously was the lodge to an estate. Calcula-
tion indicated to me that the lodge must be in the policies of
the ruined mansion I had spotted from the ridge. A woman
was hanging out some washing in the little garden which
surrounded the cottage.

I walked forward and wished her good morning, this for the
sake of getting into a conversation which I hoped would tell
me something of the history of the house and how it had come
to be in such a sad state of decrepitude. I began by asking her
whether she would tell me where I was.

'Fell Bottom,' she said. 'This be the lodge to Fell Hall and over yonder 'ee'll come to Fell Church if 'ee go fur enough. You be a stranger in these parts, then?'

'Yes, from London. I'm staying in Strode Hillary.'

'Oh, ah.' She began to peg out a sheet, but had difficulty with it in the wind, so I put down my ashplant and went to help her.

'That must have been a very beautiful house,' I said.

'Oh, ah, one time, before the fire.'

'Who owns it?'

'There's a lawsuit on. My man and I, us do be acting as caretakers, like, under Mr Okeford, who have the job of sorting things out between them as claims the property and them as wants to buy it, but there's a lawsuit on, been on for years, on and off. That foreign gentleman who bought Paine's place want the first option on it, but until they know who it belong to, Okeford can't let Winters sell. You take a look round, if you want. A gentleman like you won't do no harm. I never go up there myself. My man see to all that.'

'I'd very much like to look round,' I said, 'but I have to be getting along. Where will this path bring me out?'

'In Breedy's farmyard if you goes fur enough. Mind as how his dogs ent loose. They'm none too friendly with strangers, though all right if you know 'em.'

'Thanks for the warning.' I saluted with the ashplant, which I had retrieved, and strode on. It occurred to me to wonder whether Breedy had been the man with the gun and the retriever, but there was little point in surmising. I also wondered whether a description of the young man on the bridge would have brought any information about him, but it was too late to think of that. The woman had gone indoors and, in any case, I had told her that I must be on my way. As I walked on, I tried to explain to myself my reluctance to explore the old house. I certainly was not pressed for time, for I had told Mary that I should not be in for lunch, so I had the rest of the day before me, and the chance to poke about in a fine old place such as Fell Hall was not to be missed.

I passed a tumbledown hovel which must have been another of the lodges. Two stone pillars which had served as gateposts were still standing, but the gates had been removed. I walked

past the crumbling lodge and entered the drive. There was still
a chance of looking over the house, and this time I decided to
take it. If I encountered the caretaker again, I would explain
my reappearance on the plea that I had lost my way, but, with
any luck, I should not run into her again, for the two lodges
were at least half a mile apart.

The drive was bordered on either side by rhododendrons.
They grew wild everywhere in the county, although variety of
colour was only to be found in gardens. There were no flowers
so early in the year, but fat buds gave promise of plenty of
blossom to come in a few weeks' time.

Where the rhododendron hedges gave out, the drive curved
past lawns and then across the front of the house and took a
long slant back (I supposed) to the lodge where the caretakers
lived. Tyre marks, which I had noticed already, were deepest
in front of the house, as though a lorry had stood there, and
the tracks looked fresh.

The house no longer had a front door, but the opening was
sheltered by a pillared portico beyond which it was unlikely
that rain would penetrate. I glanced around, and then went
up the steps and entered the house.

The traces of the fire were evident everywhere. Cracked and
blackened walls and ceilings bore witness to the devastation
which must have occurred. It seemed likely that the mansion
had been uninhabited at the time. That being so, it was
difficult to imagine how the fire had started, unless it had been
the work of vandals or village boys out for mischief or a tramp
who had lighted a fire which got out of his control.

I wandered from room to room, but it was the same story
everywhere I went. Beautiful plasterwork, painted niches,
massive doorways by which the downstairs rooms opened out
of one another were all defaced, blistered or partially or even
totally destroyed. The blaze must have been visible for miles
around, but the fire brigade, if it had been called out at all,
had been called out too late to save the interior of the house.

The floors, of course, were bare and there was no furniture,
but sets of muddy footprints, still fairly fresh, which skirted
blackened floorboards and appeared again on the stairs,
seemed to indicate that the staircase itself had suffered less

damage than some other parts of the house and was safe enough to bear my weight, so, exercising caution, I mounted. I could think of no reason why anybody should have wanted to climb the stairs unless he was actuated by the same curiosity as my own, for a tramp, surely, would have been content to doss down on the ground floor. The visitor could have been the caretaker himself.

The bedrooms seemed to have suffered less damage than the downstairs rooms, although the floors here and there were perilous and I began to test my steps before venturing further. The muddy footprints were fainter on the first landing I came to, but I noticed slight traces of them on the narrower staircase which mounted to the second storey.

'Why not?' I said to myself. 'If somebody else could get up there safely, so can I.' But before I mounted I explored the first-floor rooms. Some, I deduced, had been bedrooms originally, but one of them was so grand that it must have been the ballroom. The ceiling, scorched and blackened though it was, still showed traces of elaborate plasterwork not to be matched even by the ornate ceilings down below, and the fireplace was a masterpiece of variously patterned marbles, ugly in its grandeur, but impressively conceived and executed.

There were loose floorboards and some holes. I trod carefully and did not venture very far into the room. Then I climbed the narrow staircase to the second floor and here a surprise awaited me. One of the rooms was locked and the padlock, which was on the outside of the door, was new. I examined it closely and wished I had a bit of wire with me, for it would have been easy enough to pick such a lock. It was of an everyday simple type and as a romantic boy I had made myself an expert in picking locks just for the fun of it.

I went down the stairs and looked round when I reached the pillared portico, but there was nobody about, so I took to the drive again. Suddenly I heard the sound of a vehicle. At this, I dived in among the trees and took cover to watch it go by. Rightly or wrongly, I knew not which at the time, I connected it with the locked room. It was an estate car, but I could not read the number plates because they were, front and back, plastered with thick black mud. There were two men in the car. I wondered whether one was my suicidal friend of the plank bridge, but the car went by too fast for me to recognise anybody in it.

To team up the estate car with the locked room may have been a foolish and ill-conceived connection to make at the time, but it turned out later to be entirely reasonable. At any rate the locked room fascinated me. I thought about it all the way down the long drive and wondered what secret it hid and whether the woman at the lodge knew about it.

When I was back on my track I soon found that it wound steeply upward. I took it slowly until I was looking down on the farm that the woman had mentioned. It lay at the bottom of a narrow valley and on the other side of it there was another steep hill.

I thought of a further climb. I thought of the farmyard dogs who were all right if you knew them. I wished I had the one-inch map with me. Without a map to guide me, there was no choice except to go through the farmyard and take a chance with the dogs or to turn back. I was doubtful about the former, but disinclined for the latter. For all I knew, the young man on the bridge might have decided by this time that the stream was deep enough for his purpose. I had no mind to be the person who discovered and was obliged to report his demise.

I was still standing there, looking down on the farm buildings, when sounds behind me caused me to turn round. Over the crest of the hill came a small pack of beagles and, running with them, a bevy of boys in running-vests and shorts and a couple of young men – their schoolmasters, I supposed – who were acting as whippers-in and bringing up the rear.

'Safety in numbers,' I thought; and, as they passed me, I joined discreetly in the hunt at the rear of the runners. There was no sign of the farmer's dogs as we all streamed past the farmhouse and a battered car which stood outside it, and when the beagles and their foot-followers had veered off to the left across a field, I dropped into a walk and continued along my track, toiling up and over the hill and dropping down through woods until I reached a main road and a signpost.

The signpost was of the helpful kind and gave the mileage as well as the direction, and I found that I was only two miles from Strode Hillary. I quickened my pace and in just over forty minutes I was in the market square and opposite the Stag hotel in time to get my lunch there. It was steak and kidney pie that day, and until I began to tuck in I had not realised how hungry I was. I had a pint of their special brew with my meal and left the inn greatly refreshed.

I felt I had done enough walking for one day, so headed for Innes's house. I hoped he had finished his writing, for I was anxious to give him and Mary the story of my walk and particularly to tell them about the locked room at Fell Hall and the prospective suicide on the bridge, but in case Innes was still busy I did not ring the front-door bell, but went along the side of the house in the expectation of finding the back door unlocked.

It *was* unlocked, as somebody else appeared to have discovered, for I almost collided with him as he attempted to make his exit and I my entrance. I could hear Innes's typewriter clacking away as I opened the door and as there was no sign of Mary or the charwoman I assumed that Mary was upstairs with him and that Mrs Platt had finished the chores and gone home.

I cannot say that I registered these things consciously at the time, any more than that I asked myself why a young workman, whatever his business, was under no sort of supervision. However, I remembered that I was a townsman and that they do things differently in the country.

I did notice that the young man was wearing a knitted affair which we used to call a Balaclava helmet and that it hid most of his face. I began to ask what he was doing in the kitchen, but he spun round as soon as he saw me, blurted out (in a thick voice muffled by the Balaclava which covered his mouth) something about the sink and the cooker, as he snatched up a large bag and sped out into the hall. The next thing I heard was the front door being slammed.

I rushed into the hall, but by the time I got the front door open a car was halfway down the road and too far off for me to get the number. Mary came to the top of the stairs.

'That you, Mike?' she called down. 'We've nearly finished.'

'You've had a visitor,' I said. She came down the stairs.

'A visitor? Oh, that would be Wally Halstock,' she said. 'Tidying up the garden, was he?'

'No, he was in your kitchen.'

'That doesn't sound like Wally. Of course he's often been in the kitchen, but only when I ask him in to give him a cup of tea and a piece of cake. I shouldn't have thought he would ever come in on his own. He isn't quite right in the head and he's very shy. For the first week or two he wouldn't even come inside the kitchen for his tea. We used to give it him outside the back door.'

'He said he had come to look at the sink and the gas cooker. Then he made a dash for it out of the front door and I think he made off in a car.'

'None of it sounds like Wally. What did the man look like?'

'Young, I would say, and sturdy. He nearly knocked me down when I opened the kitchen door.'

'It sounds as though he panicked. That would fit Wally, but so it would fit an unauthorised intruder,' she said. 'You know, Mike, I still don't believe Wally would have come into the kitchen unless I was there and asked him in. When the man spoke to you, could you understand him?'

'Oh, yes. He mumbled a bit through a knitted helmet, but what he said was quite clear, although it hardly made sense. Surely, even in these parts, the same chap doesn't look at sinks and gas ovens, or does he?'

At this moment Innes came down, carrying a large envelope.

'I can catch the post if I take this to the post office at once,' he said. 'Hullo, anything cooking between you two?'

'We think we've had an intruder,' said Mary. 'Mike found a man in the kitchen.'

'Wally Halstock?'

'We don't think so, and you know, Innes, there have been several burglaries around this part of the country lately.'

'Only at the stately homes.'

'Well, you have to go near the police station on your way to the post office. When you've sent off your article I wish you'd just call in and have a word with the Superintendent. Tell him it *may* only have been Wally, but we're not sure. You know

Hallicks pretty well, so he won't mind being bothered. I don't much like the idea of an intruder, and Wally has an impediment, whereas Mike says this man spoke clearly.'

'All right, then, I'll just take a look round if it will ease your mind, but I still think it was Wally. He was probably looking for something to eat.'

'If he was, he had collected it in a pretty large bag,' I said. Innes remained unimpressed. He had a good look around the kitchen, came back and said:

'Nothing disturbed in there, so far as I can see. If there was an intruder, Mike caught him in time. I'm sure there's nothing to worry about. Well, I'll be off, or I shall miss the post. I'll have a word with Hallicks on my way back.'

However, after he had gone, we found that there was something to worry about, after all. We carried the tea-things into the dining-room and Mary missed a good set of prints. She rushed into the drawing-room and found that her Meissen mirror had gone. Shocked and dismayed, she said:

'I'd better see whether anything else is missing. I wish Innes had had a proper look round before he went.' She went upstairs, but soon came down again. 'They didn't find my jewel case and your necklace and earrings, or the ring my godmother gave me,' she said. 'There was some silver in the sideboard, mostly modern, but we had an eighteenth-century teapot and a set of slip-top spoons. Innes's bronzes were in there, too. You've never seen them because he bought them quite recently. He was going to show them to you after dinner the other day, but your present to me rather took the wind out of his sails. He said he'd save the bronzes until they could have the glory all to themselves.'

She went to the sideboard cupboard. I went with her. She opened the cupboard door, shut it again and straightened up. In silence we went back to the kitchen for the rest of the tea-things. She filled the electric kettle and then we sat side by side on the settee in the drawing-room and waited for Innes to come back.

'But who would have known we had anything worth stealing?' she asked. 'All the silver has gone, and the bronzes too.'

'You will have shown people the prints and the mirror, and I expect the silver comes out on state occasions, doesn't it? People talk about these things and the information gets to the wrong ears. What are these bronzes you mentioned? Anything special?'

'Innes thinks so. One is a shepherd milking a goat. It's probably by a pupil of Riccio and a copy of the bronze in the Florence museum. The other is a girl athlete, possibly Atalanta, and so much in the style of Matteo Olivieri – there's a very similar one in the British Museum – that Innes thinks it's genuine. These Old Masters did sometimes repeat themselves.'

'How big are the bronzes?'

'Oh, quite small, really. Eminently portable, worse luck! The shepherd is only ten-and-a-quarter inches high and the running girl is smaller still, only seven-and-a-quarter inches. Of course they are both insured, and so are the teapot and the spoons, but that's not the point. Innes loved his bronzes and I can hardly bear the loss of my mirror.'

'I've a good solid shoulder and an available lap, if you want to cry,' I said. This made her smile, as I knew it would. 'And the thief has only just got away with the things,' I went on. 'The police can hardly have been alerted more quickly. I'm sure they'll pick him up soon. I hope Innes has told them a good strong tale.'

'According to the reports of other burglaries in the neighbourhood, there are at least two men involved and perhaps three,' said Mary. 'I think they may be amateurs, because fingerprints have been found. You know that Innes is on the Bench. He gets to know things like that from Superintendent Hallicks.'

'Fingerprints aren't much use unless they're on record, though,' I pointed out, 'and if these chaps are amateurs their dabs won't be on record, will they?'

CHAPTER 4

THE MAN-TRAP

Before we could tell him our bad news, Innes, whom Mary went into the hall to meet, said at once:

'That wasn't Wally Halstock in the kitchen.'

'We know,' said Mary. 'Brace yourself for an unpleasant surprise.'

'Don't tell me! We've been burgled, I suppose. If it wasn't Wally, it was a burglar. What's gone?'

'The prints, the silver, your two bronzes and my Meissen mirror. Nothing else, so far as I know.'

'Oh, well,' he said, 'that's bad, but might be worse. Thanks to Mike, the police are already on the job.'

'How can you be so sure it wasn't your gardener?' I asked, and I followed them as Mary led him to the dining-room and drawing-room and pointed to the empty spaces on the walls and to the sideboard cupboard. He said nothing to her, but answered my question.

'Apart from the fact that Wally would not dream of robbing us, he couldn't have been here when you found that chap in the kitchen,' he said. 'He's been helping the police since just after eleven this morning and he's still with them. He was on his way to a house on the other side of the valley when, in the woods, he found a man caught in a man-trap.'

'I thought they were illegal,' I said, suddenly remembering the boy on the bridge with his 'spring-guns and man-traps'.

'Of course they are! This one was probably stolen from the folk museum ten days ago. Before that, a Victorian doll went and, with the man-trap, some sets of handmade cottage-industry buttons, a swingle and a couple of early nineteenth-century handmade smocks.'

'What's a swingle?'

'What it sounds like. You swing it to beat flax so as to get the woody bits out. It's a kind of flail. Come to think of it, you could give somebody a pretty nasty knock with one, if you decided to use it as a weapon. It's made of wood, but it stands to reason that the loose part you swing must be heavy, or it wouldn't do the job it's made for.'

'Are they still in use?'

'I have no idea. Museum pieces only, nowadays, I should imagine. I don't even know whether they grow flax in these parts.'

'These smocks which were stolen would have been made of linen.' said Mary, 'the same as sheets always used to be. You can't do proper smocking on cotton.'

'Smock-frock is the full title,' I said. 'The garment was a sort of overall and the smocking was to gather the top part so that it fitted the wearer round the chest while allowing plenty of movement from the chest downwards.'

' "He knows it all!" ' quoted Mary admiringly. 'What do the police want us to do about our burglary?'

'Keep the doors locked and the windows shut and report any suspicious circumstances, that's all, but I don't suppose we'll have any more trouble. They seem to have got what they came for.'

'And Wally Halstock?'

'They've still got him, as I said. One thing: the fellow Mike found in the kitchen must be something like Wally to look at – about the same age, anyway, if that's anything to go on.'

'My description would probably fit a score of men aged between twenty and twenty-five. I only got one really good look at the fellow before he took off,' I said.

'But you would recognise him if you saw him again?'

'Only if he was wearing the same clothes, I'm afraid, and if he'd taken off the Balaclava helmet I doubt whether I could recognise him at all. I can understand about the things taken from here,' I went on. 'They were valuable; but what about the museum specimens? What use would they be to a gang of thieves and receivers?'

'Collectors' items, I suppose. I daresay there's a market for such things in America. Anyway, it seems clear why the man-trap was taken,' said Innes. 'Do you think, if you heard it again, you would recognise that man's voice, Mike?'

'I can't be sure. He only said he wanted to look at the sink and the gas cooker. As the same man seldom does both, I suspected he was up to no good. Besides, what he was carrying didn't look like a tool-bag.'

'If Wally was going to do some work on the other side of the valley, the woods would have been on the sheikh's estate,' said Innes. 'I wonder who got caught?'

'Perhaps the sheikh doesn't know that man-traps are illegal,' said Mary. 'I suppose he's been suffering from poachers. There are deer on that estate.'

'If he suffered from anything of that sort, it would be cattle rustlers,' said Innes. 'A lot of that has been going on.'

'Not in these parts, though.'

'Well, Hampshire is only over the border, and what are fifty miles or so nowadays in a car? Did you have a good walk, Mike?'

'Yes,' I said, 'and I hit upon a little bit of a mystery. Do you know Fell Hall?'

'Well, we know where it is, but we've not been there.'

'A woman who lives at the lodge – well, at one of the lodges – told me it was all right to go along and have a look at the ruins. I didn't particularly want to bother at first, but when I came to another lodge, an unoccupied one, I changed my mind.'

'What was the mystery?' asked Mary.

'A padlocked room on the second floor.'

'I expect it's where the family keep the skeletons,' said Innes.

'How about a burglar's hidey-hole for the loot until they can get it to a fence?' I suggested. I said it only as a joke, but Mary took it seriously.

'They'd need somewhere, wouldn't they?' she said. 'I think the police ought to know about your locked room, Mike. Wouldn't it be nice if we could get our things back straight away, and other people get theirs?'

We told her it was a crazy idea, but nothing would satisfy her except that Innes and I should go to the police station and make a report. She was so insistent that Innes, who, of course, adores her – so do I, for the matter of that! – said, 'Come on, Mike. We shan't get any peace until the boss has her own way.' So he got the car out and we drove to the police station and asked to see Superintendent Hallicks. I felt rather foolish, and I doubt whether the police would have been impressed by my story, let alone have decided to act on it, had not Innes been on the local Bench and Chairman of it when Lord Maumbury was not available. As it was, Hallicks listened with respect to what I had to say and to my delight (for men belong to the sex which never really grows up) the police not only got out a car, but invited us to follow them to Fell Hall if we wanted to see what was in the locked room.

'We don't need a warrant to search a derelict house,' said Hallicks.

My walk had seemed a long one, but this time we went by the way on which I had returned and the two cars made nothing of the journey. I told my brother about the two men I had seen in the estate car, and added that one of them, I thought, could have been our burglar, but I knew this was wishful thinking and rather unlikely.

However, it was not unlikely at all. The police soon sorted out the padlock I had longed to have a go at, and there before us was Aladdin's cave, or an 'Open, Sesame'.

'Of course we shall have to hold all this stuff for identification,' said the police superintendent, 'so if you recognise your own bits and pieces, Mr Lockerbie, this is a *cache* of stolen property all right, and we're taking formal possession of it pending enquiries.'

'You might stretch a point and let me have my wife's Meissen mirror,' said Innes. 'You know what women are. They are lost without their reflection in a looking-glass and she values that particular mirror highly.'

'It is a valuable piece, I'm sure, sir.'

'Sentimentally regarded, as well as intrinsically valuable, Superintendent. Do let me have it. After all, you would not have been told about this room unless she had insisted. As mere males, my brother and I would have taken the view that, if people choose to lock up a room in their house, it's their own business.'

'Ownership of the house is in dispute, Mr Lockerbie. That's why your good lady did right in being suspicious of a locked room, and in a ruin at that. Anyway, if you were to slip the mirror to your brother while my back is turned and he were to decide to nip downstairs and put it in your car, I don't know that anybody need be the wiser.'

Mary was delighted to get her mirror back. It was a delightful piece, a long, rather narrow oval with a pair of naked infants at the top. Down the sides were roses and carnations, each porcelain creation slightly different from any other, and every petal as exquisitely modelled as were the tiny hands and fingers of the *putti*. I think there were tears in Mary's eyes as she hung it in its place again. She said, 'Oh, Mike, thank you,' so, despite Innes's presence, I kissed her. He did not mind. He smacked me between the shoulder-blades when I had released her, and said, 'Great stuff, old man, and all done through ornery curiosity, eh, you snooper?'

'I don't know about curiosity,' I said, 'but I hope the police will go easy on that woman at the first lodge. She can't have any guilty knowledge, or she would never have suggested that I should go up and take a look at the house. She said she never went there herself.'

'Perhaps one of the men in the estate car is her husband. If so, he probably knew something, even if she didn't,' said Innes. 'I find it hard to believe that the caretakers had no knowledge of that locked room. Surely it was their responsibility to keep an eye on the house to make sure it wasn't vandalised? Not that we get much of that sort of thing around here, although somebody did set fire to the village school once, so Martha Lorne told us, but that was years ago.'

'Fell Hall is so badly damaged already that any vandalism would hardly be noticed,' I said.

I thought that, so far as I was concerned, my little adventure was finished, for I was due to return to London after the weekend, but on the day after my visit to Fell Hall Innes received an invitation from Lord Maumbury for Innes, Mary and myself to dine at his house on the Wednesday of the following week. A woman member of the Bench was to partner me, and the others begged me to stay on in Strode Hilllary and accept the invitation.

'I've nothing to wear,' said Mary, as women always declare on these occasions.

'Your blue,' I said. 'I love you in that.'

'With Mike's trinkets,' said Innes, 'or had you forgotten them?'

'There is a dinner gown at André's. I saw it when you were buying a book in Bristol last week. It would set off the necklace and earrings beautifully. If we went today, perhaps they haven't sold it yet,' she said.

'You won't get it if I don't like it.'

'You *will* like it. Shall we go?'

So off they went. I was invited to accompany them, but women's dress shops are no longer in my line, and I preferred to stay back and find my own amusement while they were gone. Scarcely could their car have turned the corner when a female newshound from the local paper rang up. She understood that I could give her a story, so might she call?

'Mr Lockerbie is out,' I said.

'Aren't you Mr Lockerbie?'

'That's my name, but I'm Michael Lockerbie. I'm a guest in the house.'

'May I call in about half an hour? I've read your books.'

Well, I had no plans except to go out for some lunch later on, although Mary had told me there was plenty of food in the kitchen, so I agreed to see the girl, although to a male reporter I think I would have given the bird. She turned out to be a very pretty girl, neatly dressed in a dark brown frock with long coat to match, and she even wore a hat, although she soon removed this and tossed it on to the settee when she had taken an armchair.

I did not think Innes would grudge her a glass of his sherry, so I got it out and we settled down. She began by producing her credentials and then spoke flatteringly about my books.

'Perhaps you'll bring Fell Hall into the next one,' she said brightly. 'Oh, it's all right. I've been to the police to get their story and they referred me to you. They don't care how much publicity the story gets. They hope it will turn up an informer.'

I gave her my story, such as it was; she asked a number of questions which I answered as well as I could, and then I thought it was my turn.

'What about this man-trap business?' I said. 'Do you usually go in for these anti-poaching devices in these parts?'

'It's likely to turn out nasty for at least two people,' she answered soberly. 'The victim's leg may turn gangrenous. He's got head injuries, too, and he may die. The hospital is doing all it can. I've been there, of course, but you know what they're like; they won't tell you a single thing if they can help it, but even if they amputate the leg it may not save the boy's life. I gathered that much. If he dies there will be a manslaughter charge, I suppose.'

'Murder, perhaps. Man-traps and spring-guns are highly illegal, and nobody can argue that there was no intention of committing bodily harm, because, obviously, there was. I mean, you don't set a man-trap for nothing. Strangely enough, a young man I met when I was out walking mentioned man-traps and spring-guns.'

'That sounds like guilty knowledge. Who was he?'

'I have no idea. The victim of the man-trap, by the way, surely ought not to have been in the woods if they are preserved?'

'That part of the estate is not preserved and, anyway, he had every right to be in the woods. His father owns them. The victim is the second son of the sheikh. You've heard of our sheikh, I suppose?'

'His son? Good Lord! At what time of day is it supposed to have happened?'

'Late in the evening, they think, and, of course, he wasn't found until well after breakfast-time on the following morning.'

'Wasn't he missed?'

'No. He's at university and the family wasn't expecting him home.'

'I wonder why he decided to go home, then?'

'Nobody knows yet. Even when he recovers consciousness – if he does – it will be some time before he can be questioned, the hospital told me.'

'What was he doing in the woods, anyway?'

'Taking a short cut from the station, or so it's thought. He was involved in a car crash some time ago and has been banned from driving for a year, so they suppose he came by train and decided to walk the rest of the way.'

She took herself off at about eleven and I went upstairs to find myself something to read. Innes has a considerable library and I had no doubt that I could hit upon something light which would keep me occupied until I was ready to go out for a snack and a drink. I picked out *Huntingtower* and *John McNab,* both old favourites of mine, but as, downstairs again, I turned the pages, I soon decided that neither Dickson McCunn's Scottish Presbyterian conscience nor Palliser-Yeates's chivalry would suit my mood. After all, I had had my own little adventure and had no need for others at second hand.

I returned the books to their shelf and looked out of the library window. It offered the same view as that from the adjacent bedroom, for both were at the back of the house and overlooked the garden, the paddock, the church tower and the hills. Suddenly a fancy took me to see for myself the scene of the man-trap crime. The man-trap itself would no longer be there, but perhaps I should be able to make out the spot, for the man-trap would have been hidden on one of the tracks through the woods, no doubt, and the ground round about it trampled by the police and others. If anybody challenged me as a trespasser I would claim that I was a stranger and that I had seen no warning notices. My car was in the road, for Innes did not possess a double garage. I took my ashplant, got in and drove to the railway station, as that seemed the obvious point from which to begin my exploration.

As I approached the station, it occurred to me that a young man coming home by train would have had some luggage with him, and as, even by taking the short cut through the woods, he would have had a two-mile walk ahead of him to reach the house called Bourne Farley, which Innes had told me about and which was marked on the Ordnance map, he would hardly have burdened himself with luggage to carry.

Enquiring about this at the station might open up a talking point with a porter or, better still, the ticket-collector, I thought.

I parked the car and went into the booking hall. There was a ticket-collector at the entrance to the platform. Apparently a train was expected. I addressed him.

'Is there a left-luggage office here?'

'Apply at the booking office, sir.'

'Thanks. Sad about the young Arab prince, eh?'

'That's as may be. Them as sets snares got no quarrel if they get caught their own selves.'

'You mean he himself set that man-trap? That's impossible. He would have known it was there.'

'Then his dad set it. They lot be heathen savages, I wouldn't wonder, and up to all manner of wickedness.'

'Did you see the young man get off the train?'

'And collected his ticket off him, as be my duty. First class it was. Money like water they foreigners got.'

'Did he have luggage with him?'

'Not many as travels first class is without luggage.'

'I suppose he left it with the booking clerk.'

'Being as it was two suitcases and a bag of golf-clubs, reckon he did. He couldn't hardly get it all through the door here, which I had to take his ticket from between his teeth, he was that loaded.'

'Isn't there a station taxi he could have taken, instead of leaving his luggage and going off on foot?'

'Ben Plush was otherwise engaged.'

'What does that mean?'

'He was engaged by Mr Okeford, who skip out of the six o'clock train quick and took up Ben Plush afore anybody else could get a look in, that being Mr Okeford's way, and not a thought for anybody else's convenience that might like to share Ben Plush with him. Lawyers is a selfish kind of bodies, to be sure.'

'Was the young man disappointed at not getting the taxi?'

'Said a few words in his own language, I makes no doubt.'

'And dumped his luggage in your booking office, and went off on foot, only to get caught in that wretched man-trap, it seems. I wonder who it was really meant for if his father had had it set?'

'What you after, mister?' He looked at me out of suddenly hostile eyes.

'Oh, nothing. Couldn't his father have sent a car to pick him up?'

'That ent no business of mine.' The sound of the approaching train interrupted our conversation. I went to the booking-clerk's window, but a couple of travellers, women intent on a day's shopping in Exeter, no doubt, were taking their tickets and were having an unheated but persistent argument with the clerk about cheap day-returns. No doubt the train would wait for them. That was still one of the pleasant things about country branch-lines and country buses. Only country lawyers, it seemed, were disobliging. I did not wait to make any enquiries about left luggage, but returned to my car and drove into the village to find a pub.

Over my pint I asked the barmaid whether it was possible to take my car through the woods to reach Bourne Farley House. I had business there, I stated mendaciously. She summed me up before she answered my question and then, instead of replying to it, she said she supposed I was 'one of they newspaper gentlemen from London'.

'No,' I said, feeling that, as I had told one lie, I might as well follow it up with another on the principle, I suppose, that if you have committed one murder you may as well commit another because the punishment (especially true of hanging) will be the same. 'I am a solicitor and, yes, I do come from London.'

'They'll need you up at Bourne Farley,' she said. 'Setting them nasty man-traps! Serve 'em right as it was their own boy got caught. God's justice, that was, I reckon.' Then she answered my question. 'You can't get through them woods, not any road at all now. Barred 'em right off, they have. Police and that.'

I soon discovered that she was right. When, after a short interval devoted to trial and error, I found the entrance to the sheikh's woods, it was not only most effectively barred off, but a policemen was on guard at it.

At the sight of him a kind of small-boy spirit entered into me. I would do no harm in the woods, I said to myself, I would keep well clear of any trampled soil or broken undergrowth. I would return by the same way as I had gone in. (I would need to do so in any case, in order to get back to my car.) I would keep to the paths, break no branches, do no damage of any kind, but I wanted desperately to get into the woods. I drove sedately past the policeman and looked ahead and slightly to my right in search of a possible entrance.

The lane, like all the side-roads of that countryside, wound in curves and bends, so that a couple of hundred yards took me beyond the point at which the policeman could still see the car. I slowed down to ten miles an hour, still keeping a look-out on my right. Soon the lane ran between high banks, so I stopped the car on a convenient patch of grass, got out and climbed the right-hand bank. I had left the confines of the trees behind me. From the top of the bank there was nothing close at hand but scrub, dead heather and seedling pine trees, but eastward I could see the woods.

There seemed no reason why I should not leave the car where it was. It was off the road and in nobody's way. I struck out for the woods, taking a long slant which would bring me well to the rear of the policeman on guard duty.

It was not easy walking. I caught my foot now and again in heather roots and sometimes had to thrust my way between bushes. This meant that I had little attention to spare for my general way ahead. After a bit, I decided that I had better stand and take my bearings, so when I came to a patch where the scrub thinned out, I stopped and looked ahead. I was within a hundred yards of the woods, but between them and myself were two picturesque but, to my mind, menacing figures. In full rig-out of Arab head-dress, flowing garments and carrying heavy sticks, were two enormous black men apparently on guard over the woods on the open side.

Although they did not appear to carry guns, I deemed discretion the better part of valour. I walked northwards over the heather, keeping level with the men but not getting any nearer to them, and then I made a long cast westwards and made my way back to the lane and my car.

I drove on until I could find a place to turn. This was provided by a farm gate where the heather and scrub had given way to pasture. When I came in sight of the policeman I was half-inclined (for I was chagrined at being baulked of my intention of entering the woods) to stop and tell him that two men in fancy dress (probably intended as a disguise) were acting suspiciously along the western borders of the woods, but I thought it would be better not to draw attention to myself by pulling his leg, in case I had another chance to get into the woods later on.

CHAPTER 5

ENTER A GODMOTHER

'Well, you might have expected it,' said Innes, when I gave him and Mary an account of my morning. 'Naturally the police don't want a crowd of sightseers tramping all over the woods and destroying possible clues. Woods are usually damp, especially at this time of year. Whoever set the man-trap must have left footprints. Once those are identified, there's an open and shut case.'

'Gamekeepers, poachers, picnickers, the village kids? There must be dozens of footprints,' I said.

'Perhaps it's as well you were not able to add yours to them,' said Mary. 'I'm going up to put on the new dress and your necklace. You may both tell me what you think about the effect, so long as it's complimentary.'

'I promise not to mention dogs' dinners,' said Innes. When she had gone upstairs he said, 'While she's out of the way I'll tell you something, Mike, that I don't want her to know until I'm sure that it's going to come off.'

'Know what? What doesn't she know?'

'That I've persuaded Hallicks to let me send for her godmother. I don't want Mary to know until I find out whether Dame Beatrice can come.'

'What's it to do with your police superintendent whether she comes or not?'

'He doesn't like this man-trap business one little bit. He thinks some of the local toughies have gone a lot too far. There is considerable local feeling against Abdul, as I told you, and Hallicks believes the man-trap was set in the hope that somebody would get caught in it and that the sheikh would then be in trouble for having such a thing on his land. Not that he would have had any idea it was there, I'm sure of that.'

'Why is he in such bad odour? It can't matter to the local lads that he bought Bourne Farley.'

'Oh, it isn't mere prejudice, and it's very strong. For one thing, a number of people lost their jobs up at Bourne Farley when Abdul bought the property. He replaced the indoor staff with his own retainers. Then, nobody likes his bodyguards or the way his sons race about on motorbikes and in fast cars. The previous owners were pretty easy-going, but the sheikh has brought several lads up before the bench for poaching. I believe I told you how somebody always pays the fines. Anyway, Hallicks says he wouldn't be a bit surprised if young Hamid was decoyed into those woods with the intention of springing the trap on him.'

'So why Dame Beatrice?'

'Because, although Hallicks has his suspicions, he's got no proof. Dame Beatrice is consultant psychiatrist to the Home Office, so I've suggested that she should be asked down here ostensibly on a visit to Mary and me, but actually to vet his suspects. He isn't in a position to charge anybody in particular, you see, but there are four young fellows he thinks might know something about the man-trap. He doesn't want to pull them in officially until he's got something more than a mere hunch to go on. If the sheikh were British and a local favourite, he would risk it, but, as things are, he needs a good reason for asking anybody to show up at the police station just for questioning, and, under the circumstances, I don't blame him. Even the police have to tread carefully in some cases.'

'So you suggested letting Dame Beatrice have a go, she having no local connections.'

'Yes, so, if you'll excuse me, I'll get her on the phone while Mary is out of the way. If I know anything about women, it will take Mary at least three-quarters of an hour to get her hair right and her face right and put on that gown and the accessories.'

He came back looking pleased.

'So Godmother is going to play ball?' I said.

'Yes. I've just rung Hallicks and told him.'

A little later Mary came down in the new dinner-gown. It was flame-coloured and set off the jewellery extremely well, I thought. When we had admired the effect she went upstairs again and came back wearing a kaftan, the most graceful of garments, in which she looked seductive and beautiful.

'Did you really see Abdul's bodyguards?' she asked. 'Or did you make that up?' Without waiting for an answer, she went on: 'You know, Mike, I don't understand why young Hamid – yes, that's his name; the eldest son is called Selim and the younger ones are Omar, Suleyman and Murad – why Hamid ever decided to walk home through those woods that evening. It sounds quite out of character. That Arab lot go everywhere on great big motorbikes and in fast cars.'

'It was because the solicitor, Okeford, had bagged the only taxi, so the boy had to walk, I suppose,' I said.

'There is a telephone at the station. He could have rung up Bourne Farley and got his father to send a car. The sheikh has a whole fleet of them and, apart from the chauffeur, all the sons can drive except the youngest. People see them breaking the speed limit all over the place.'

'Perhaps he had an assignation in the woods.'

'That is what I wonder. He could have been decoyed there, don't you think?'

'All I think is that I wasn't prepared to argue with those two plug-uglies who were patrolling the outskirts of the woods, or that policeman on the gate. He might have suspected me of trying to remove the evidence of the crime.'

'She is coming,' said Innes. 'She suggested next week, but yielded under pressure and she'll be here to lunch tomorrow.'

'Well, there's only one "she" in your vocabulary,' said Mary. 'Are we to expect my godmother? If so, you'll have to take us all out to lunch tomorrow because it's much too late for me to order anything from the butcher today and it has to be something special for my godmother.'

I had never met Dame Beatrice and had never seen a photograph of her, so I was unprepared for the little, thin, black-eyed, witch-like being who came in a chauffeur-driven limousine at eleven-thirty on the morning following my abortive attempt to enter the sheikh's woodland.

The chauffeur was to return to Wandles Parva, the

Hampshire village where Dame Beatrice had a house on the edge of the New Forest, and to come back to Strode Hillary to pick her up when she sent for him. She supposed that that would be in a very few days' time, since her assignment was to assess Superintendent Hallicks' suspects, pinpoint the guilty one, if he existed among them, and then return either to London or to the Stone House. She also wanted to take a look at the patient, the unfortunate young Hamid, for she was a doctor as well as a psychiatrist. I believe it is the rule nowadays that a psychiatrist has to be both.

Superintendent Hallicks had been invited to lunch with us and, to avoid too much local gossip, it had been decided that we would not patronise the Strode Hillary hotel, but drive out into the country to a place which had an excellent reputation for its cooking and where there was a good chance that we should not run into anybody who knew us or who would be inclined to speculate upon our being accompanied by a police officer.

We took both cars. Innes had the superintendent and Dame Beatrice in his and, to my great pleasure, I was left to convey Mary, for, although there would have been a seat for her in Innes's car, she refused to allow me to be odd man out and make the trip alone.

'What do you think of my godmother?' she asked as we drove off towards Paulet Marquise on our way to the sea.

'Terrifying. I feel like making the sign to avert the evil eye every time she looks in my direction,' I said. Mary laughed.

'You must have a guilty conscience, then. She's the kindest, most understanding person I've ever met,' she said.

'Understanding? Yes, that's what I'm afraid of. She looks right through me and decides that I am what Brutus called a "slight man". I feel that I'm ticketed as a non-starter.'

'I hope she'll find the Super's culprit for him. He's worried about that man-trap. Coming on top of that pot-shot somebody may have taken at the sheikh himself, Hallicks is afraid of a real outbreak of violence. After all, this part of the world did produce the Tolpuddle Martyrs, so there's plenty of determination below the surface of these apparently easy-going people. They've taken a scunner at poor old Abdul, and once they've got a notion into their obstinate heads, it would take a bulldozer to get it out again. Two girls, at different times, have run away in two different villages, and haven't been traced yet, so, of course, in the opinion of the locals, they are now ornamenting the women's quarters at Bourne Farley.'

'Likely, do you think?'

'Heavens, no!'

'How can you be so certain?'

'Abdul was educated over here. He is completely westernised, and so are his sons.'

'Don't you believe it! They never are. The veneer of a public school and Oxbridge soon wears off when they get back to their own environment. The Koran allows them four wives and, I suppose, any number of concubines. How many sons do you say he has?'

'First and foremost, he isn't back in his own environment, and his sons are Selim, Hamid, Omar, Suleyman and Murad. Selim is in the Middle East now, looking after the oil; Hamid is the man-trap victim, Omar and Suleyman are at Eton and Winchester respectively, and Murad is still at prep. school – *this* prep. school, incidentally, so he's a day-boy and lives with his father at Bourne Farley.'

'Well, I'd take a five-pound bet that some of them are only half-brothers.'

'Oh, I don't think so. They are nicely spaced. Selim is twenty-five, Hamid nineteen, Omar seventeen, Suleyman fifteen and the little one is eleven or twelve.'

'You seem to know a lot about them.'

'There is an English housekeeper and she is a member of the W. I. That's another proof. I don't believe the highly respectable Mrs Liddon would work in a house where there was a consortium of wives and slave-girls, especially if some of the concubines were kidnapped village children.'

'Perhaps you have a point there.'

'I rather wish he *did* have a harem. I'd love to know what goes on in them.'

'Gossip, scandal, back-biting, jealousy, hysteria, plotting and scheming, the exchange of lewd jests, boredom and, as opportunity arises, poisonings,' I said.

'You might have lived in one!'

'Not I. Women in the mass confuse me.'

For the rest of the journey, which did not last nearly long enough to suit me, we talked similar agreeable nonsense, and all too soon I had to pull up in the forecourt of a fine old Tudor house turned into an hotel. The lunch was good and Superintendent Hallicks obviously enjoyed it.

Nothing was said about the real purpose of the outing until we were taking coffee in the lounge. Then, setting down his cup, Hallicks came to the matter in hand.

'I've got four youths I'd like you to see,' he told Dame Beatrice. 'One is a tearaway, not from these parts, who works at a local garage, another is so thick that he might think a man-trap was a good joke without ever considering the pain and danger to anybody caught in it, the third is a recognised psychopath who ought to be in an institution, and the fourth is a chap who was sacked from his gardening job up at Bourne Farley for stealing expensive fruit and blooms from the hot-houses and selling them. He was lucky not to have been prosecuted. All the same, I expect he's got a chip on his shoulder because of losing his job.'

'I shall not be prejudiced by your answer to a question,' said Dame Beatrice. 'Do you suspect one of the youths more than the others?'

'If there is any guilt among those lads, I might suspect two of them of being in collusion, ma'am, the psychopath and the stupid chap. The former would have thought of stealing the man-trap and the other one would have been talked into doing the actual donkey-work of setting it.'

'But neither has any known grievance against the sheikh?'

'Nothing that has ever come to light, but nobody likes the old gentleman very much.'

'What about the gardener who was dismissed? You indicated that he nourishes a grievance.'

'He talked a lot, mostly in the pub, but I don't really think he'd do more than talk. Another reason why I suspect the psychopath is that the local curator has given him a job as cleaner at the museum, so he was in a stronger position than the others, perhaps, to steal the man-trap.'

'But it is the ex-gardener who has a reputation for stealing? I see. Was the man-trap the only stolen article?'

The superintendent mentioned the smocks, the buttons, the swingle and the doll which had been stolen earlier.

'But that's another thing,' he said. 'We reckon the boarding school had the smocks and the swingle. The smocks had been rigged up as a couple of scarecrows and put in Farmer Breedy's field of winter wheat. We fixed on the schoolboys because there was a notice pinned to one of the smocks which read: BEWARE. THE BLACK HAND STRIKES AGAIN.'

'What about the swingle?' asked Innes. 'Could young Hamid's head-wounds have been inflicted with that?'

'No, Mr Lockerbie. As a matter of fact, we found the swingle when we found the shirts. We reckon whoever burgled the museum soon chucked everything away except the man-trap. We reckon some of the boarding-school lads found the things and set up the shirts on the scarecrows. They had wired the swingle on to the sleeve of a shirt. The school lads had a feud on with Amos Breedy on account of his guard dogs setting about one of their beagles, but I thought that was all over.'

'Oh, *those* boys!' I said. 'Breedy's farm wouldn't be near Fell Hall, would it?'

'Not so far from it, sir.'

'I went through the farmyard with the boys and their masters, who were following the beagles, on the day that I discovered the locked room. There was no sign of any guard dogs. So the boys took their revenge, did they?'

'Well, being young gentlemen and not vicious, they were pretty careful where they trod among Breedy's young corn and not a lot of damage seems to have been done, considering. Breedy reckons the slogan was a threat and wanted us to go to the headmaster, but Breedy has been a nervous sort of man ever since there was a nasty accident when a car ran into his lorry nearly a year ago, and somebody got killed and others injured. He keeps two Alsatians as guard dogs because he's afraid the party in the wrecked car have got it in for him, although Breedy was exonerated from any blame for the accident.'

'Local people?' asked Innes.

'Unfortunately, yes. The dead man was a Mr Lorne. Anyway, the track through the farmyard is a right of way, and Breedy has no business to keep savage dogs on it.'

'Lorne?' said Innes. 'I suppose you don't mean Martha Lorne's husband?'

'That's right, sir.'

'Strange. We know her quite well, but she has never mentioned that her husband was killed in an accident.'

'Rigg Halstock, his son Walter and that chap Winters were the others in the car. Winters was driving and the car went out of control and hit Breedy's lorry. Young Walter got a pretty good knock which has left him a bit short in the top storey and with a speech impediment, and Rigg Halstock had an arm amputated and lost his job because of it. He used to be head gardener to Lord Maumbury, but, of course, a one-armed gardener isn't any sort of use, so Maumbury got him a job as caddy on Clypthampton golf course and helped him out with a small pension which, if you ask me, the Maumbury estate can't really afford, so I reckon the noble lord acted very decent, considering that the accident was nothing to do with him. *Noblesse oblige,* as they say.'

'Is it certain that the farmer was in no way to blame for the accident?' asked Dame Beatrice.

'There was a witness, and this is where I don't like the way things are going, ma'am. The witness was young Mr Hamid Aziz, the victim of the man-trap. He swore to the car going out of control. In any case, Breedy himself wasn't driving the lorry. It was parked.'

'I see. So my examination of your local troublemakers is really designed to establish their innocence, is it?'

'I would not put it quite like that, Dame Beatrice. It's more a matter of clearing the rubbish out of the way. I wouldn't put it past any one of those lads to have set that man-trap out of pure boneheadedness and mischief, but there *is* that other matter, and Rigg Halstock is still a very bitter man. These chaps brood on things a long time before they act.'

'A one-armed man could hardly set a man-trap,' said Dame Beatrice.

'True enough, ma'am, but I think he and Winters could

have planned it together *and* enticed young Hamid into the
woods that evening with a faked letter from a girl, or
something of that sort. I don't know whether, when you've
talked to the village lads, you'd like to tackle the boarding
school?'

As we should have to pass the turning to Lower Gushbrook
and Hallicks had put no time limit on the hours he would be
spending with us, I asked Dame Beatrice whether she would
like to see the picturesque mere and the baby trout-stream.
Hallicks thought well of the idea.

'Not our most picturesque village, ma'am,' he said, 'but the
surroundings are real pretty and it would be a pity, as we're in
the neighbourhood, for you to miss the view. Any landscape
with water is real nice, I always think.'

So Innes took the Lower Gushbrook road and Mary and I
followed in my car. When we reached the village, Hallicks and
Innes remained in their car, Mary and I got out of ours and
Dame Beatrice joined us. As Mary and I had done on our
previous visit, the three of us strolled upstream, passed by the
ancient, rotting punt and crossed the tiny clapper bridge to
look at the island.

On our return I halted by the punt and looked at it in some
surprise. The wild plants I had pointed out to Mary had all
gone, but had been replaced by others, and the whole sodden
surface had been beautifully tidied up, as had the ground in
front of it.

'What are you staring at, Mike?' Mary asked.

'Look for yourself. The plants have been changed,' I said.
'Who on earth would have bothered?'

'Village children, of course,' she said.

'Leaving this beautifully tidy surface? I don't believe it,' I
retorted.

'Some school project, perhaps, of a botanical nature,' said
Dame Beatrice. 'That would explain it, would it not?'

'They must be well-disciplined kids to have made such a
very neat job of it,' I said. 'Quite the professional touch, I
would have thought.'

When we got back to his car it was to find Innes and
Hallicks deep in a discussion of the car crash which had killed

Lorne, so no mention was made of the punt, and Mary and I
went back to my car and we drove home.

'So Lorne was killed, Halstock senior lost an arm, Halstock
junior lost some of his marbles and young Hamid gave
evidence that no blame attached itself to Farmer Breedy and
his lorry,' said Innes, when we got home. 'What's your verdict,
Mike?'

'An open one,' I replied. 'I would have thought most of the
resentment would have been directed against Winters, who
was the driver of the car, especially as he appears to have got
off without injury.'

'Oh, I expect his licence was taken away. He never drives
anywhere now,' said Mary. 'Besides, there was that potshot
from among the trees when he was talking to the sheikh. You
said it must have been meant for Winters and not Abdul, if
you remember, Innes. You produced chapter and verse.'

'Yes. I said that if you shot at the sheikh you couldn't miss
him.'

'How dangerously you Dorset people live! I had no idea,'
said Dame Beatrice.

'It's been quiet enough in Strode Hillary until now,' said
Innes. 'Perhaps we've been placidly existing on top of an
active volcano, but I can't really think so.'

'It follows the usual pattern, I expect,' said Mary. 'Years go
by and nothing happens, and then something triggers matters
off and, before you know where you are, the skies are falling.
After all, it took only one crazy individual to start up the 1914
war.'

'So a shot was fired in the sheikh's grounds,' said Dame
Beatrice, 'and the shot went through somebody's hat.'

'That could have been accidental. A chap could have been
out shooting and bagged the hat instead of a pheasant or a
rabbit, I suppose,' I said.

'Hardly a pheasant,' said Innes, 'and it must have been a
very tall rabbit if the shot went through Winters's hat.'

'Gamekeepers have guns,' said Dame Beatrice. 'Why were
the sheikh and Mr Winters in conference in the open air?' she
added.

'The sheikh has his eye on some land he wants to acquire. Winters does land-deals of a rather shady sort,' said Innes. 'They were probably on their way to look at Long Fallow.'

'So, in order of occurrence, as I understand it,' said Dame Beatrice, 'we have a car accident in which one person was killed, two others injured and from which the driver of the car, although the accident can be attributed to him in that he allowed the vehicle to get out of control, escaped without injury. Then, of course, we have a shot, a cache of stolen goods and a youth caught in a man-trap.'

'The brakes were faulty,' said Innes. 'That came out at the inquest, according to what I have been told. It all happened before we came here, of course, so I know nothing except by hearsay. We know the woman whose husband was killed, but she has never mentioned the matter to us and until now I had not heard the name of the dead man.'

'That seems somewhat strange, does it not? Do you know the woman well?'

'In a way I suppose we do,' said Mary. 'She is a member of the W.I. and so am I. She comes here now and again for cocktails and occasionally, but less often, we go there. She was prepared to be kind and helpful when we first moved into this house, so now it's very difficult to dislodge her, as we told Mike, and we don't want to seem toffee-nosed, of course. The trouble is that she really isn't our sort.'

'I see. She is not an acquaintance you would choose to have if you could avoid it. What about this feud between Farmer Breedy and the schoolboys?'

'I can't imagine it's very important,' said Innes. 'The boys are children of twelve and thirteen. It's only a prep. school. They may have set up the scarecrows, but the man-trap is a different matter entirely. Are you going to interview them when you've seen Hallicks' hobbledehoys?'

'I do not recognise class distinctions,' said Dame Beatrice, leering hideously at Mary. 'I would like to find out whether they saw the man-trap when they purloined the smocks and the swingle, that is all.'

'Does it matter whether they saw it?'

'I think it might. If they did not see the man-trap when they found the rest of the loot from the museum, I should be inclined to think that the man-trap was the object of the exploit and that the other things were taken under the false impression that they would act as a blind. Again, of course, one must not lose sight of the possibility that the thefts from the museum were merely an act of bravado, that the goods were thrown away as being too compromising to keep, and that then somebody who had nothing to do with the theft discovered the discarded man-trap and used it.'

CHAPTER 6

FOUR AND THREE

There was plenty of daylight left. It turned out that I achieved my object after all, and that by the simplest means. Dame Beatrice had told Hallicks that before she talked to his suspects she would like to be shown the spot where the man-trap had been placed. Innes, in his capacity as a local magistrate, added himself as of right, with no objection from the Superintendent, whom we picked up at the police station directly after tea, and I tagged along, hoping that my presence, although it could hardly go unnoticed, might at least be tolerated.

We went in two cars, a policeman driving the one containing Hallicks and Dame Beatrice, Innes driving his own with me beside him. We went first to Bourne Farley, where we stopped while Hallicks went into the house for a short courtesy visit to the sheikh. I was in hopes that Abdul the Bulbul would join us, but this did not occur. Hallicks came back alone and the cars traversed a long drive across the home park to where the trees thickened and we entered the woods.

Here, in a clearing, we parked the cars and left the police driver and made the rest of the journey on foot. I suppose we walked at least a mile over the residue of the autumn leaves and past the brilliant spring greenery of hawthorns, before, at another clearing, Hallicks led us along a miry little path, much trodden but so narrow that our shoulders brushed the bushes on either side of it, and we ended in another clearing. Here, footprints were everywhere.

'This is the place where Wally found Hamid,' said Hallicks. 'There's nothing much to see, Dame Beatrice, except all the footprints – mine and my chaps' mostly, of course, but we did check those of Hamid and Wally.'

'The clearing seems a good way from the main path through

the woods,' said Innes. 'I wonder what caused young Hamid to come here? I quite expected the trap would have been set on the main path.'

'The most mysterious thing, to my mind,' I said, 'is what Hamid was doing in this neighbourhood at all, even in pursuit of female society. I thought he was at college. The university term can't be more than a week or two old.'

'His father is expecting a letter from the Dean of his college, sir,' said Hallicks, 'as I learned when I called on him just now.'

'Oh, really? What about?'

'Young Hamid must have been sent down from college, he thinks, and was fooling about in the woods killing time because he was afraid to go home and tell his father what had happened.'

'Good Lord! Doesn't sound like the present generation, does it? – afraid to tell his father, I mean.'

'Seems that young Arabs may have more respect for their fathers than some of our lot, sir. Well, here we are.' He drew aside a piece of sacking. 'Those are the outlines of the implement, Dame Beatrice. There seems to have been no attempt to hide it. Makes me wonder whether the lad was in the woods a lot later than we thought and stepped on the contraption in the dark.' He replaced the sacking and we walked back to the cars.

I was puzzled. If Hamid had got off the six o'clock train, he must have hung about in the woods for a very long time before he stepped on the man-trap, for it did seem more than likely that he had done so after dark. A young man as well-heeled as the sheikh's son might have been expected to kill time at a hotel, or he could have left the train at Ropewalk and gone to a cinema to get through part of the evening, and met the girl far more conveniently that in miry woods at that time of year. The sun did not set until just after eight o'clock, so he could have been in the woods for the better part of two hours before he stumbled upon the trap if he had not spent time elsewhere.

Dame Beatrice was to see Hallicks' suspects that same evening.

'I may be able to dismiss one, probably *only* one, of your suspects from any subsequent inquiry,' she said, 'but I think it will take a longer time and more than one session before I can make a confident prognosis.'

The lads were Jed Poole, the garage hand, by reputation the bad boy of the neighbourhood; Wally Halstock, written off as 'thick' by Hallicks, but actually brain-damaged by the car-crash, son of the now one-armed Rigg, who had been injured in the same accident; Peter Chettle, called by Hallicks a psychopath (but with what authority I did not know); and Ernie Batcombe, the young gardener sacked from Bourne Farley because he had stolen exotic fruits and hot-house flowers and sold them. Left to myself and what I would call juryman's commonsense, I would have opted for the last of these boys as the man-trap setter.

Hallicks had suggested that either Innes or myself should sit in at the interviews. 'Dame Beatrice is elderly and frail,' he said. I thought of those claw-like hands and the beaky little mouth, the brilliance of the eyes and the unnerving cackle of sardonic laughter, and thought it was as well that Dame Beatrice was not present to hear his words. 'If one of those lads was to turn ugly,' he went on, 'I wouldn't give the old lady much chance.' As I could write shorthand ('Good, sir. That will give an inoffensive reason to both parties for your presence at the interviews.') I was the man selected to be a squire of dames – in this case of *the* Dame. She, however, refused to entertain Hallicks' plans for her protection.

'I am not accustomed to have anybody else in the room when I am at work,' she said, 'and until I can be sure that these young men are guilty and have to be turned over to the police, they are sacred and my patients.'

'They themselves may not see it that way,' I argued; but she was adamant and we had to give in. That the lads did not see it 'that way' was obvious from the beginning. They were self-conscious, resentful and suspicious. Hallicks' assurance that none of them was under suspicion of having set the man-trap and that, so long as they told the truth, they had nothing to fear, had hardly the result of reassuring them.

However, they were sufficiently obedient to his authority and (or so I thought) sufficiently the victims of their own guilt-complexes to assent grudgingly to his suggestion that

they should be interviewed separately by Dame Beatrice. He
pointed out that there was no need for them to answer any of
Dame Beatrice's questions if they did not wish to do so, that
they were in a private house and not at the police station, and
that neither His Worship (Innes) nor himself would be present
at the interviews. As Dame Beatrice had already decided that
this applied to me, too, when the boys had been given pork pie
and beer in the kitchen and three of them had settled down to
watch television, Wally Halstock was conducted to the library
to be interviewed.

The evening was a long one. This was not because Dame
Beatrice took all that much time to question each youth, but
because the boys were not willing to abandon any television
programme in which they were interested. We got through, in
fact, only when the late film ended and they had finished all
that remained of the beer.

'Of course I can't use any of your findings officially, Dame
Beatrice,' said Hallicks, 'but if there is anything I can follow
up ... ?'

'There is one thing,' she said, 'which may interest you. The
man-trap *did* catch the person it was meant to catch.'

'Which of them told you that?'

'None of them, in so many words, but in a day or two I shall
be in a position, I hope, to substantiate what I say.'

'Are they all involved?'

'You may dismiss the garage hand, young Jed Poole, from
your calculations, I think, and I would also exonerate your
gardener.' Her last interview had been with Batcombe. She
had been told about the thefts from the hot-houses, of his
summary dismissal by orders of the sheikh, and of the fact that
since his dismissal he had been unemployed. She gave us an
account of the interview.

'Do you go to church, Mr Batcombe?'

'Course I do. Sing in the choir, don't I?'

'From your voice I deduce that you are a powerful baritone.'

'That's right.'

'You know your catechism, no doubt.'

'Used to. You have to know it to get yourself confirmed.'

'Ah, yes. "To keep my hands from picking and stealing—" '

'Come off it! That's old hat, that is!'

'So you seem to have proved lately, but there *was* a time ... '

' 'Tain't right some should have it all and others nowt.'

'I'm afraid it is the way of the world, but no doubt you thought you were right in attempting to adjust matters to some limited extent.'

'The old buster never took me to court. I'll give him that.'

'Perhaps he sympathised with your sociological motives.'

'Come again?'

'Who set that man-trap, Mr Batcombe?'

'You asked him outright?' exclaimed Mary.

'I might have expected this question to evoke a spirited response,' said Dame Beatrice, 'but, to my great satisfaction, Batcombe looked down at his powerful, countryman's hands, then at me again and said:

' "Everybody know that, but I don't reckon nobody be going to squeal."

"When you worked for the sheikh, how did you get on with his sons?" I asked him.

' "I never see much of 'em 'cepting the little 'un what live at home all the time. Nice little chap. Learnt me to acrobat like he says the beggar kids does in his country, although him being a sort of a kind of prince, he weren't supposed to play with 'em, but he says as all men be equal in the sight of the Prophet. He said as Allah the All-Merciful, the All-Compassionate, made all men equal, and a lot more of that sort of heathen stuff. I learnt him how to imitate bird-calls and how to make a whistle out of a bit of reed, and how to put a ferret down a rabbit-hole, things like that. I like the little beggar."

' "You still meet?"

' "Now and then, when he haves a half-day off school."

' "Does his father know?"

' "I reckon so. Offered me me old job back so long as I kep' out of the hot-houses, but I does better on the dole and got me time to meself."

' "On taxpayers' money!"

' "Somebody got to spend it for the gover'ment, ain't they?"

' "You are an extremely immoral young man."

' "Not me. You got to get a gal into trouble to be that. The Reverend tell us so." '

'So you think that, if for no other reason, you ought to find Batcombe innocent on account of his churchgoing?' asked Innes, grinning.

Dame Beatrice cackled and replied that we are all whited sepulchres, some whiter than others. In Batcombe's case his churchgoing proved nothing. 'If you remember,' she said, 'there was the ex-pirate Ben Gunn, who could rattle off his catechism so fast that you could not tell one word from another.' She went on to say, 'Of course, I am assuming for the present that I have made the right deduction and that the man-trap caught the person it was meant to catch. If this proves not to be the case, I must abandon my theories and rethink the whole business. I could do with more data, but I doubt whether much more information will come from these young men. Whatever Batcombe's faults, I absolve him from any desire to inflict bodily harm on Hamid.'

'Why have you exonerated Poole?' asked Mary.

'To explain that would be to give you an extremely boring technical exposition,' Dame Beatrice replied, 'so I will say only that, although I cannot compel people to tell me the truth, there are certain tests which indicate that a patient is lying. I applied these tests and they convinced me that Poole knows nothing about the purloining or the setting of the man-trap.'

'Innes and Mary are convinced that Wally is also in the clear,' I said.

'If he had not a father, I would not have troubled to question him,' said Dame Beatrice. 'I would like to meet Halstock senior. He may be a very vengeful man. He lost an arm in a collision with Breedy's lorry and Breedy was completely exonerated from blame owing to the eye-witness account given by this young Arab who has been caught in the man-trap. Moreover, Wally Halstock suffered brain damage in the same accident, and his father may resent that as much as he may resent his own serious injury.'

'If you are right, wouldn't you think Rigg Halstock would have it in for Breedy more than for Hamid?' I suggested.

'Yes, indeed, and for Winters, who was the driver of the car,' she agreed. 'I do not think we are anywhere near the end of this affair.'

'Sounds like a bloodbath,' said Innes, looking uneasy.

'Of course, the man-trap incident may have nothing at all to do with the car crash or with the unpopularity of the sheikh. We must keep an open mind. Meanwhile, I want to talk with the small boys who rigged up the scarecrows in Farmer Breedy's field,' said Dame Beatrice.

'Breedy does seem to figure rather largely in all this,' I said. 'What did you make of Jed Poole, apart from exonerating him?'

'I think he is capable of making a nuisance of himself when he feels like it, but I gathered that he seems to find his daily work congenial and, so far as I can tell, far from having a grudge against the Arabs, he benefits from them to the extent that any overhauls to their cars are carried out at the garage where he is employed and he also supplies their many vehicles with petrol. He has received numerous *pourboires,* it seems.'

'How about Chettle?' asked Innes. 'I gather that you don't feel inclined to dismiss him from your calculations.'

'Not altogether. If nothing more, I think he may well figure among those who (according to the youth Batcombe) know who set the trap, but who are not revealing any names. I also think he stole it from the museum, but at someone else's instigation. I may need to see him and Batcombe again, but not until I have talked to young Hamid.'

We left it at that. She then telephoned Hallicks. He promised to see that the schoolboys responsible for setting up the scarecrows were available for questioning and rang up later to tell her that the headmaster had agreed that the boys should be questioned, but that the interview must take place at the school with himself or a senior member of his staff present. Hallicks added that he had arranged for me to accompany Dame Beatrice, as my shorthand notes, when transcribed, might be valuable as a record of the proceedings in case of subsequent doubts about what had actually been said, or if there was any trouble with the boys' parents.

I gathered from this that the headmaster had been difficult, but when we got to the school nothing could have been more urbane and courteous than his reception of us. He was kind enough to say that he knew my work, and his manner towards Dame Beatrice bordered upon the obsequious. He gave us armchairs in his sitting-room and, remarking that the boys would talk more freely if he made himself scarce, he left us and a moment or two later a man in a track suit ushered in three boys wearing the school uniform of grey shorts, green blazers and grey sweaters.

Introductions were made, I retired into a corner with my notebook (a pad of ordinary stationery provided by Innes), the young master took an armchair and the boys were given seats. They were self-possessed young gentlemen and betrayed nothing of the mixture of embarrassment and alarm which, at their age, I myself would have felt in similar circumstance. In spite of their cherubic countenances and (or perhaps because of) their poise and good manners, I wrote them off as villains and hoped that Dame Beatrice would not be taken in by them.

She asked them their names and inscribed these in her own small notebook. They were Tarrant, Ashmore and Stanbridge and they turned out to be the president, the secretary and the junior treasurer of the school club which owned and followed the beagles.

'It's thought better to have a master to take charge of the subs and the outgoings and all that,' the child Stanbridge explained, 'so my job is to make sure the men pay their subs and I write to the parents with bloodsucking letters to get more money, and all that kind of thing. There's quite a lot to do, actually.'

'Bloodsucking letters?' Dame Beatrice enquired.

'Asking people to sponsor us and saying *mens sana* and how the club gets chaps out into the fresh air instead of frowsting in the dayroom or guzzling at the tuck-shop, you know.'

'Admirable. Less admirable, perhaps, to trample fields of young corn.'

There was a moment of silence, then the president spoke.

'We didn't really *trample* anything. We put up the scarecrows almost on the edge of the field. We wouldn't *trample* anything.'

'It was a *gesture*,' explained the secretary. 'We took a very poor view of his Alsatians. There's a right of way through the farmyard and our hounds are all under control because, of course, they are only interested in the aniseed, and as our trail-layers stick absolutely to public land, there's never any trespassing. As for hares, well, we're conservationists. There's no hunting, or anything like that. It's just the aniseed.'

'Mr Percival would soon disband us if there was trouble. He threatened to do it over the scarecrows, but Mr *Kingsley* Percival – ' he glanced at the long-legged, track-suited young man in the armchair '—Father Williamed him out of it.'

'So disaster was averted,' said the secretary, 'but we have to watch our step. We could have thought up something much more effective than the scarecrows if Breedy had gone on trying to bar us the way through the farmyard, but, anyway, there are too many other things to do and he's more reasonable now.'

'So it is not only for *idle* hands that Satan provides mischief,' said Dame Beatrice. 'However, it is not your sins which concern me, but the means whereby you committed them. The scarecrows, I gather, were suitably, although burglariously, clad.'

'We didn't *steal* anything,' said Tarrant. 'Honestly we didn't. We *found* the things when we were setting the course for the beagling.'

'Ah, yes. You *found* the things. We approach the heart of the matter. Perhaps Mr Ashmore and Mr Stanbridge will kindly exclude themselves from the gathering while I have a word with Mr Tarrant.'

The schoolmaster took the two boys out and closed the door behind them before he returned to his chair. Dame Beatrice addressed herself to the remaining child and, observing pleasantly that he was not upon oath but that the matter was one of importance, she asked him where the stolen smocks had been found and what else had been found at the same time. She received the answer which I myself had expected. The swingle had been found and appropriated by the boys as a suitable adjunct to the smocks, the card of buttons had been caught on a bush nearby and adjudged as of no interest, the doll received no mention – perhaps it was beneath contempt, I thought – and the boy said nothing about the man-trap. She sent him off, and Mr Kingsley Percival, whom I took to be the headmaster's son, brought in Ashmore and, when he had been dismissed, Stanbridge was brought before the inquisitor. The answers remained unhesitating and constant. The exact locality of the finds and the finds themselves were described by each boy in turn, but, until she came to the junior treasurer – the writer of bloodsucking letters to parents (I could not help wondering whether the headmaster knew anything of this particular activity) – she did not unleash the sixty-four-thousand-dollar question.

'And what did you do with the man-trap, Mr Stanbridge?' she asked in the casual tone she had used throughout the interviews. For the first time one of the little boys forsook his calmness.

'Oh, look,' he almost squeaked, 'we didn't do anything with the man-trap, really honestly we didn't! It wasn't there. We didn't do anything with it. It just utterly simply *wasn't there!*'

'And the doll?' Dame Beatrice enquired.

'What doll? We didn't see any doll. What would we want with a doll?'

'Did you get what you wanted?' I asked as we returned to the house.

'At any rate I got what I expected,' said Dame Beatrice. 'Naturally it would never enter my head that those little boys would have *set* the man-trap. I should suppose them to be physically incapable of doing so, even if I thought it their kind of mischief, which I do not. I am of the superintendent's opinion that the thefts from the folk museum were directed towards the purloining of a cruel and dangerous device and that the thief or thieves hoped that adding the other items would disguise the real object of the enterprise. I think the superintendent may have to look hard at young Chettle – even harder than I thought when I talked to the youth.'

'There are still the chaps from the school,' I said. 'Little boys can be stupid and cruel, don't you think? They may have set the trap for a lark. Of course I don't mean for an instant that they *stole* the items, only that they found them and planned mischief with them.'

'It can be argued that stealing by finding constitutes an offence, and that would apply to the swingle and the smocks, but I am sure they did not find the man-trap when they came upon the other objects,' said Dame Beatrice.

'What about the missing doll?' I asked. 'Was it considered such a despicable object as to be unworthy of mention by the boys?'

'The card of buttons was mentioned. I don't think the boys found the doll,' said Dame Beatrice. 'I was told that they did not, and I believe them.'

'I've seen it in the folk museum,' said Mary. 'They only had the one. I have never seen one quite like it. It is a home-made Victorian doll dressed as a snowman. I would have loved it when I was a child.'

CHAPTER 7

BEATING THE BOUNDS

The interviews with the schoolboys had begun at just after nine o'clock, so we had arrived home again at soon after ten. Mary slipped out after she had made her remark about the missing doll and I found myself wondering whether I had been right in assuming that the boys had found it. After all, if Mary's description of it was correct, as I had no doubt it was, it was not any ordinary doll and surely, if the boys had seen it with the other purloined museum specimens, it need not have been admitted by them. It might have been appropriated as a mascot or a curiosity which they had no intention of giving up.

I spoke of this to Dame Beatrice and she observed that my speculations were interesting and that she would ring up young Mr Percival and ask him to press the point with his pupils. This he promised to do and said that he would ring her back. He was as good as his word and within half an hour she had his assurance that the boys had seen nothing of the doll.

Innes, without waiting for Mary's return, poured the mid-morning drinks for himself and us, and the conversation turned on to the procession which was to take place on the morrow.

'I trust,' said Dame Beatrice, 'that it is not proposed to beat the boys as well as the bounds?'

'No,' Innes replied. 'No claim to territory is involved. This is a religious ceremony directed towards blessing the farms and the crops.' He looked out of the window. 'The weather report is nothing special. If it rains I shall persuade Mary that there is no point in our joining the procession of cars. It will only mean mud all over the windscreen and the wipers going all the time. I hadn't really thought of joining in, but last night she said she would like to take part.'

'Where has she got to?' I asked.

'Shopping. She's a long time gone. I expect she's run into somebody she knows and has been roped in for a gossip. That's the only drawback in a place of this size. Everybody knows everybody else and you're considered very odd and stand-offish if you don't stop for an exchange of news and views.'

Mary came back bearing her sheaves, so to speak. Having dumped her parcels, she settled herself to tell us the news.

'I met Mrs Sydeling and Miss Upcerne in the Square. Winters has disappeared,' she said.

'Absconded with the church offertory box?' asked Innes ironically. 'That wouldn't surprise me in the least. The man's a villain. I expect he owes money all over the place.'

'You've no right to say that,' said Mary. 'You have nothing whatever to go on.'

'There's his face, there's his manner, there's his loathsome little moustache and there's the shot which went through his hat.'

'Miss Upcerne thinks that was meant for Abdul. It's so much more likely, in spite of what you say. Local feeling is still very strong about Bourne Farley going to an Arab.'

'They should blame the vendor, not the purchaser.'

'His sister is rather worried, but thinks it's too soon to report it to the police. He has stayed out before, and she would think nothing of it except—'

'Whose sister are you talking about?'

'Winters's sister, of course. She has kept house for him ever since his wife walked out.'

'First I knew that he ever had a wife. Do you get all the local dope at those afternoon meetings of the W.I.?'

'Not at the meetings, darling. We're much too busy. Members chat when we meet in the town, of course. That's how most of the news comes everybody's way sooner or later.'

Innes got up and poured more drinks and the conversation was switched back again by Dame Beatrice to the Sunday procession. Innes took the opportunity of sounding Mary on the subject of the weather.

'I thought you had made up your mind not to go,' she said. 'I didn't think the weather came into it.'

'That is not what you said last night. If you want to go, we'll go, unless it pours with rain.'

'Perhaps Dame Beatrice would like to take part,' said Mary.

Dame Beatrice disclaimed any such desire on the grounds that she felt inadequate at religious festivals.

'I suppose bad weather will not deter the faithful,' she said.

'Only to the extent that the little services will be held in barns instead of in the open air,' said Mary. 'I do hope the weather holds up, though. The route goes through some of the loveliest countryside in Dorset, and that's saying something. I always wonder why any of us go for holidays when there's everything one could wish for right here on the doorstep, but Innes can't do without at least a fortnight in his beloved Scotland. Anyway, I thought tomorrow's thing might be rather fun. It starts off miles from here. In fact, Strode Hillary is nearly halfway along the route. The procession of cars meets in Ropewalk high street and from there it comes in our direction and stops first at a dairy farm to bless the herd, then at a fruit farm, after that comes a riding-stables and then there is the stop for tea at Paulet Marquise.'

'Tea?' said Dame Beatrice. 'This is not a morning procession, then?'

'No. It kicks off officially at three-thirty, giving everybody time to attend morning church, eat Sunday dinner and do the washing-up,' said Innes. 'They will allow an hour for tea at Paulet Marquise and then visit a sheep farm just outside the village. After that they will re-form in the market square here and go on to a trout farm. We saw the beginnings of the trout stream at Lower Gushbrook. Then the cars end up at Aries St. Peter, where there is a short Church service and then refreshments at the vicarage for all those who have stuck it out to the end. Most people will, I expect.'

'It all sounds most delightful,' said Dame Beatrice.

'But not quite your cup of tea? I'll tell you what I suggest, then. Let's take the main route, as we did before, leaving out visits to the farms, and show Mike some more of the countryside, as we planned. I'll book Sunday lunch in Ropewalk, leave Mary at the hotel while I drive you and Mike home, Dame Beatrice, and then I can get back again for Mary by the time the procession of cars begins to assemble. How would that suit everybody?'

Mary, however, turned the plan down. She said she no longer wanted to go on pilgrimage. This was just as well, for scarcely had we got indoors, after lunching at Ropewalk that Sunday, than the clouds darkened and the rain fell so heavily that Innes had to switch on the lights to enable him to read his Sunday paper when we returned.

'My poor daffodils are not going to like this,' said Mary, standing at the french windows and looking at the sodden tubs and their wilting occupants. 'One thing, we've had the best of them. They are nearly over for this year.'

' "When a daffodil I see

Hanging down his head t'wards me,

Guess I may what I must be," ' quoted Dame Beatrice solemnly. She went on:

' "First, I shall decline my head;

Secondly, I shall be dead;

Lastly, safely bury-ed." '

I looked at the thin, lined face, the apparently frail figure, and wondered at her calm philosophy, but, of course, said nothing of my thoughts. Mary's more robust mind was much bolder than mine. She quoted in her turn, and from the same poet:

' "Stay, stay

Until the hasting day

Has run

But to the Evensong,

And, having prayed together, we

Will go with you along." '

Dame Beatrice cackled, a harsh sound incongruent with her delightful voice when she spoke. She changed the subject.

'What were young Mr Chettle and young Mr Batcombe up to at Lower Gushbrook?' she asked. 'I noticed them as we drove through it on our way to Ropewalk.'

'Peter and Ernie?' said Innes, looking up from his perusal of the newspaper. 'Were they there? I didn't spot them. They're not usually birds of a feather, I believe, although at different times I've had each of them up before me on the Bench,

Chettle for poaching and Ernie for causing a breach of the peace by hitting a fellow member of the local Supporters' Club over the head with a mug of cider and starting a general *fracas* or, as the law puts it, an affray.'

'So you go in for football hooliganism even in these parts,' I said. 'I thought the fighting always took place between *rival* gangs of supporters, though.'

'Ernie's cousin, who plays at full back, put the ball through his own goal,' Innes explained. 'Another youth strongly criticised this action because it was the only goal of the match. His remarks caused Ernie's clan spirit to be aroused and he bounced the pint pot on the other lad's head which, fortunately for its owner, is made of teak. What annoyed him most, he explained later, was not being crowned so much as the waste of cider, for Ernie, with great presence of mind, had seized the other fan's pint with which to commit assault and battery on him.'

'Talking of Lower Gushbrook,' I said, 'I think some of the village people have been having a game with that waterlogged punt. You noticed it, Mary, when we took Dame Beatrice there the other day.'

'You pointed it out,' she said.

'You remember those plants which were growing in it?' I turned to Innes. 'Well, they'd been changed. Some had gone and the others were differently arranged and there were roots of water forget-me-not – doesn't flower for about another month, but I couldn't mistake it – and that most certainly wasn't growing in the punt when we went to Lower Gushbrook the first time. I wonder who's been gardening?'

'Oh, kids love playing games with mud and water, and making little gardens,' said Innes, 'but I would like to know what Peter and Ernie were doing there today. It's right off their beat. I hope they haven't made some mischief to upset the procession this afternoon. The church will be empty until the procession arrives, and Ernie may be a churchgoer, but it isn't *his* church.'

'But will the pilgrims go into the church? I thought it was only arranged to go straight through Lower Gushbrook on the way to the trout-farm,' said Mary.

'Well, if those two were together, they weren't up to any good,' said Innes. 'There's nothing in the paper, by the way.' He tossed it aside. 'Are there any muffins? Let's have tea early and then spend a long cosy evening thinking about how wet the procession will be. I wonder whether they'll cut things short in all this rain?'

'Not they,' said Mary confidently. 'They can't by-pass any of the farms. Offence would be taken. Besides, there is all the trouble people have gone to with the tea at Paulet Marquise and the refreshments at the vicarage.'

'I do not think country people pay much regard to rain until the rivers burst their banks and there are floods,' said Dame Beatrice. 'Snow is a different matter. It blocks roads and the sheep have to be dug out of drifts. I think Mary is right. The pilgrimage will go on as planned.'

Tidings of it came to us on the following morning. They were brought, of course, by Martha Lorne. The rain had ceased during the night and a burst of sunshine brought her along at eleven o'clock just as Innes had set out the usual bottles. He brought another glass from the kitchen and Martha settled down to tell us the tale. Her excuse for calling at such a time, she said, was to bid me farewell before I returned to London.

'That is very kind of you,' I said, 'but, actually, you know, I'm not leaving today, after all.'

'No, it *was* the arrangement,' said Mary, 'that Mike should go home after lunch today, but, now that my godmother is here, we've persuaded him to change his mind. Did you do the bounds yesterday, Martha?' (I noticed that she did not mention Lord Maumbury's invitation.)

'Well, I'd been offered a seat in the Tollers' car and I did not like to disappoint them. I knew *they* would go, whatever the weather. You know what very *Church* people they are. The daughter has her eye on the Reverend Basil. Such a mistake for a bachelor to take on five parishes. One of them is bound to have a designing spinster or two, don't you think? So embarrassing for the Reverend Basil because Gloria Toller has no reticence or inhibitions at all, but simply goes all out to make her desires *known*. Jane Upcerne has the same hankerings, but is much more discreet. Sometimes I think she'd like to murder Gloria,' said Martha.

'Talking of murder,' said Innes, 'has anything more been heard of Winters?'

'Well, he wasn't at the tea-party in Paulet Marquise church. I don't remember seeing him at Aries St. Peter vicarage, either, but of course there was such a crush there that we overflowed into three rooms, so one might have missed him. I must say that the W.I. had done a wonderful job at the vicarage. One advantage, I suppose, of being a bachelor vicar is that all the women will work their fingers to the bone for you.'

'I didn't realise that the W.I. was involved,' said Mary. 'Nobody mentioned it at the last meeting.'

'Well, there was so much other business and, in any case, all the arrangements were put in hand *weeks* ago, before you joined, dear, and all the volunteers were co-opted then, and promises given and duties assigned and all that.'

'Perhaps I ought to have turned up yesterday after all, but the weather was beastly and I have two guests staying—'

'Oh, don't talk about the weather! It was all right at Breedy's farm because we had our little service in that lovely old barn which used to belong to the abbey in the far-off-days, but only the vicar got out at Mrs Smith-Tidewell's. The rain came down in sheets and he just said a quick blessing on her ponies and a mare which had a tiny foal, while the rest of us cowered in our cars. The dairy farm was more or less all right because we all made a quick dash for the dairy itself and the cowsheds. The vicar blessed both and one of the dear cows mooed a most beautiful Amen. We had to laugh.'

'Did the W.I. do the tea at Paulet Marquise?' asked Mary.

'Oh, my dear, no! Lady Maumbury undertook Paulet Marquise, as she did last year, but some of our members *cooked* for it and it was a great success. I think people hung tea-time out as long as they could because of the rain, but eventually we got everybody back to the cars. Half a dozen youths turned up on motorcycles and were a very great nuisance and rather a danger weaving in and out and racing their engines the way they do, and all looking like beings from *Star Trek* or a horror comic or something. I believe they only came for the tea, although they did stay with us after that. One of them skidded almost under the wheels of the sheikh's car, and only the chauffeur's skill prevented a very nasty accident which would have spoilt the whole thing.'

'You don't mean the sheikh turned up in church!' said Innes.

'Not in the actual church, no. I don't think he got out of his car at any of the stops until we went into the vicarage, and that was with a purpose. The vicar has a beautiful bitch with a litter of pups – golden Labradors, you know – and the sheikh had his youngest son with him and was given no peace from little Murad until he had bespoken a puppy for the boy.'

'Did the motorcyclists attend the service?' asked Mary. 'And who was the one who skidded?'

'Oh, yes, they had grace enough to come into the church. If they had not, I don't suppose even Peter Chettle, wicked though he is and not as psycho as he pretends, would have had cheek enough to go into the vicarage for cake and cider and sausage rolls and wolf his fill. It was Ernie Batcombe who skidded.'

'Was he hurt?'

'Oh, no. The devil looks after his own,' said Martha Lorne bitterly. I exchanged glances with Innes, but, of course, neither of us made any comment. She went on: 'I don't know how he got the money to buy a motorbike. He's been out of work for months, and the bike looks brand-new.'

'I expect the State provided it, along with his board and keep,' said Innes. 'That's why fools like me pay our taxes.'

Mary thought it well to change the subject.

'Did Jed Poole turn up?' she asked.

'No. The garage was open, so I suppose he had to work. That dreadful Peter Chettle, who doesn't own a bike, rode pillion behind Ernie. So dangerous!'

'So he got spilled too,' said Innes.

'He fell into the hedge, that's all.'

'Boys on bikes are monkeys on sticks,' I said. 'No sooner down than they're up again.'

'Boys are like cats,' said Innes. 'They have nine lives. I crashed on a push-bike when I was twelve years old, and went headfirst down a hill which was littered with boulders, but I never touched one of them. Everybody said it was a miracle.'

'Well, I wish Ernie Batcombe and Peter Chettle had broken their necks,' said Martha. 'The village could well do without them.'

'Did anything happen at Lower Gushbrook?' asked Innes. Martha looked surprised.

'No. Why?'

'Because those two lads were there. I thought they might have been up to mischief as it was on the route taken by the procession. Besides that—'

'So the sheikh's little boy had one of Diana's puppies,' said Mary, making another deliberate intervention.

'Well, he *chose* one, but it is too young to be taken from its mother. He is to have it in two weeks' time. I hope he will treat it properly. Foreigners have a bad reputation for cruelty to animals. Oh, dear! Is that the time? I had better go.'

'One for the road,' said Innes. She sat down again and had one for the road. Then, as she rose to go, she said,

'Winters was not at breakfast this morning. I met his sister in the Square as I came along here. She was extremely worried and had been to the police. They are not bound to look for missing persons unless there is reason to suspect foul play, and so they told her, but she isn't satisfied, of course. After all, there was that bullet which went through Winters's hat and even if that was meant for the sheikh and not for Winters, it couldn't have been a very pleasant experience for either of them.'

'Winters may have decided to leave the neighbourhood for a bit,' said Innes. 'He was responsible for negotiating the sale of Bourne Farley to the sheikh, wasn't he? Perhaps that has made him somewhat unpopular in some quarters, and he knows it. I expect the bullet scared him into going into hiding.'

'I don't know what Strode Hillary is coming to. Bullets through hats and people caught in man-traps! I wonder how young Hamid is getting on?' said Mary. 'How soon will the police be able to question him?'

'According to what I've heard,' said Martha, 'they won't need to amputate the leg. The rumours about gangrene, even

if they were true – and I don't believe they were, because
gangrene surely would not have set in so soon – must have
been greatly exaggerated. Gloria Toller, who knows one of the
sisters at the hospital, told me that Hamid had recovered
consciousness, but, of course, she knew nothing about when
the police would be allowed to talk to him. That is a matter
for the doctors to decide.'

'What a good thing he will not lose the leg!' said Mary.
'He's only nineteen years old, I believe. It's terrible to lose a leg
at any time of life, but particularly dreadful at that age. Will
he be crippled?'

'The sheikh is so rich that everything will be done which *can*
be done,' said Martha. 'You would think the police would
have found out by now who set the trap. I heard that the
sheikh is offering a huge reward for information. Personally, I
suspect Jed Poole. He's wild enough.'

'I'm afraid you are wrong this time, Mrs Lorne,' said Dame
Beatrice. 'I am sure Jed Poole did not set it.'

'Well, somebody did,' said Martha spiritedly, 'or Hamid
couldn't have caught himself in it, could he? If you ask me,
there is something very strange going on, and everything
began with that bullet through Winters's hat. Effie Winters
was worried to death when he told her of it.'

'Would a bullet through my hat worry *you*, Mary?' asked
Innes.

'Not if you were walking with somebody else, especially if he
was known to be unpopular. I should be certain that the bullet
was meant for *him*, and I should just hope that you wouldn't
walk about with him any more.' She turned to Mrs Lorne.
'How long has Winters been missing, Martha? By that, I mean
when does his sister say he was last at home?'

'I don't know exactly, but long enough ago for her to be
worried about not hearing from him. At first Effie Winters
thought he might have seduced one of the village girls and
gone into hiding for fear of the father or brothers – not that
anybody cares much about that sort of thing these days – but
there have been no rumours. No gossip has been bandied
about, or I would have known.'

'Why did she expect to hear from him? Brothers are not all

that considerate of a sister's feelings. They seem to assume she hasn't got any,' said Innes.

'Well,' said Martha, 'Effie thought that by this time he would either have sneaked back for some clothes or asked her to send some along. She says he took nothing with him, not even so much as a clean shirt. That's what really worries her – that and the bullet, of course. She doesn't even know when he left home. She had been away for a few days, although I believe she was back for the weekend.'

CHAPTER 8

THE WATERLOGGED PUNT

One mystery soon seemed to sort itself out. The police picked up the Fell Hall caretaker, Burrows, for the local robberies, and he completely exonerated his wife, who, as we had surmised, could have known nothing about the locked second-floor room in the ruined building. However, he turned Queen's evidence on Winters who, he alleged, had been his partner in crime.

'So far, so good,' said Innes, when he heard the news. 'Well, the hearing before the Bench will be more or less a formality now. On Burrows's own confession we shall have to send him for trial. Anyway, everybody's stolen property, including our own, will soon be returned, and Hallicks will have a further reason for rounding up Winters. What is more, the hospital has now given permission for him to see Hamid, provided he does not excite or tire him. It will be interesting to know what the boy has to say.'

He met Hallicks after the court hearing at which Burrows had been ordered to be remanded in custody, but had little to tell us when he came home.

'The doctors only allowed Hallicks about five minutes with Hamid,' he said, 'and it wasn't long enough to get anything helpful out of the lad, so we're back to square one so far as the man-trap is concerned. All that came out is that Hamid has no idea how he came to step on the man-trap and has no recollection of being hit on the head. May have fainted with pain, he thinks, and got clobbered while he was unconscious. It's quite possible, I suppose.'

Innes and Mary had been in somewhat of a quandary over the invitation we had received to dine with Lord and Lady Maumbury. The invitation had included me, but not Dame

Beatrice, for she had not been with us when it was issued. It seemed equally invidious for us to make some excuse for opting out, or to put the Maumburys to the possible embarrassment of having to make an addition to their table of guests, for perhaps they would have felt they had no option but to invite her to join our party.

Tentatively Mary had broached the subject on the Friday night. Dame Beatrice dealt with it in a forthright way which drew protests from us all, but she was adamant.

'Of course you will go, and of course you will not mention that I am staying with you. No, I will *not* have Mr Michael stay at home to keep me company, kind though it is of him to offer. As a matter of fact, I have business of my own to attend to, and shall be glad of a solitary evening.'

We assumed that she had letters to write and I have no doubt that this was so at the time, but subsequent events resulted in a change of plan. While Innes was in court on the Wednesday morning and Mary was supervising the prepara-tions for lunch, Dame Beatrice asked me whether it would trouble me too much to take her over to Lower Gushbrook again and point out the plants which had been added to, or substituted for, those originally in the punt.

'You're thinking of Batcombe and Chettle, I suppose,' I said, 'but why should they have bothered?'

'Batcombe is, or was, a gardener, Mr Michael.'

'I'll run you over there, by all means, but Innes tells me there have been no complaints, so far as Lower Gushbrook village or Sunday's procession are concerned. He assumes that the two lads were not up to mischief, but were simply out for a spin on Batcombe's motorbike at the time when you spotted them as we passed through the village on Sunday.'

She looked at her watch and then went out to the kitchen to enquire the time of lunch. Mary came back with her.

'That will be all right, Mike,' Mary said to me. 'When Innes is in court I never know when to expect him. Sometimes, if they've got a lengthy session, they adjourn and have a bite in a pub. Our lunch is a casserole, so you two go off and enjoy yourselves. No need to hurry back.'

To my surprise, Dame Beatrice asked me to pull up outside

the police station. She said she had something to ask Hallicks before we went on to Lower Gushbrook. She was soon back in the car and as we drove out of the town and on to the Paulet Marquise road she said,

'The bullet through Winters's hat came from a rifle, not a shotgun. There was just one hole and the police, at the sheikh's instigation it seems (for Winters made no official complaint), searched the grounds for the missile and found it. Apparently, had the marksman lowered his sights a little, Winters would have been killed.'

'Strange that he didn't complain,' I said.

'It seems that he told his sister and that is how the news became common property. Winters seems to have thought that the sheikh was the target.'

'Innes thought not.'

'And appears to have been right.'

I did not ask her what she meant and no more was said until we pulled up opposite the mere and even then she did not speak until we were walking back alongside the infant trout-stream and were approaching the punt. Then she handed me one of the two trowels which she had taken from the bag she had placed on the back seat of the car before we started. I assumed that the trowels had been borrowed from Innes's garden shed and I deduced, from their gleaming condition, either that they were Mary's property or else that they were new and had never been used by Innes, who was lazy about cleaning garden tools.

'What's this for?' I asked. 'Are we going to add to the contents of the punt?'

'It is more likely that we are going to subtract from them,' she said. She spoke a trifle grimly, I thought. 'When we get to the punt we have to dig.'

'Dig up the plants, you mean?'

'No. Just dig. The plants must take their chance.'

But when we reached the punt she had to change her mind. It looked as though Batcombe and Chettle might have been up to mischief at Lower Gushbrook after all. When I had seen it last, the punt had presented a tidy, even a workmanlike appearance, but now the new plants were hidden under a mountain of rubbish which consisted mostly of ashes from fireplaces, together with cinders and soot, although I also noticed what appeared to be grit and sand, probably purloined from the bins which were to be found on the steepest gradients ready for use on winter's icy roads.

Dame Beatrice clicked her tongue and waved her trowel regretfully at the punt.

'I am afraid Superintendent Hallicks will have to take it on trust that the contents of the punt ought to be investigated,' she said. 'I suppose there is a post office with a public telephone somewhere in the vicinity? I had counted on our having to excavate leaf-mould and other plant deposits. I hardly think our trowels are likely to make much impression on this addenda without the expenditure of far more time and labour than we can afford at this juncture.'

'There's a public call-box near the church. I noticed it when I came here with Innes and Mary the first time,' I told her.

'If you know where it is, go to it and ring up the Strode Hillary police station. Ask them to get here with all speed and bring spades, shovels and a sieve with them. I shall stay on guard here and pretend to be sketching the scenery until you return. That will indicate a reason for my protracted presence should anybody take an interest in it, although there seems to be nobody about, and the spot is not overlooked by any of the houses.'

She was right when she said that there was nobody about. The village could have been a place of the dead. I did not see a soul until I came back to Dame Beatrice herself with the result of my telephone call.

'They're coming as quickly as they can,' I said. 'They would like us to stay here until they arrive, to make sure that nobody plays any tricks. Hallicks seemed unimpressed by my report and said that they did not expect any results from their digging, but he also admitted that he thinks a hint from you may well be worth following up. It seems that he is more concerned about Winters's disappearance than he allowed the sister to believe, or, in fact, than he himself believed at first.'

We strolled up and down, pausing at times while Dame Beatrice, sketching-block in hand, occasionally added a stroke or two to her drawing just in case somebody had us under observation – although this seemed unlikely, as there still was nobody about and that end of the mere could not be overlooked, I reminded myself. This fact became of some importance.

Hallicks, with a sergeant and two constables, turned up with the implements Dame Beatrice had specified, and they erected a screen on the shoreward side of the punt before they got to work. Hallicks had a word or two with us and then indicated, politely but unmistakeably, that our presence at the scene of operations was no longer required.

I realised later that he had taken my report so seriously that he wanted to spare us the sight of any disagreeable disclosures which might come to light. I also thought of Mary's casserole and my stomach began to rumble. One thing which Hallicks had mentioned to Dame Beatrice was that the hospital had given permission for Hamid to be questioned again and that, if she wished to avail herself of this offer, he was prepared to stand down in her favour.

That afternoon she and I went our different ways, for I had been requested to put in a little more detective work at the railway station following a call she had made directly after lunch to the sheikh's secretary at Bourne Farley. She told me that she had given Hallicks's name, proclaimed her own identity and then had asked for the name of Hamid's university and college.

What excuse she gave for needing this information I did not know, for she sent me off to the railway station without disclosing either her intentions or the object of my enquiries. I was told what questions to ask and was puzzled, since I believed they had already been answered. However, not mine to reason why.

'I shall not go to the hospital until I have received your report,' she said, as we walked out to my car. 'I need a little more ammunition before I confront young Hamid.'

It seemed a heartless way in which to refer to a bedside visit to a very sick man, but I knew that she was not heartless and that her telephoning must have been both interesting and important, so I drove off in a state of pleasant anticipation of the disclosures which, with any luck, might be coming my way.

I had been told to be as discreet as I could in questioning the ticket-collector to whom I had spoken on my previous visit.

'We do not want to arouse his curiosity,' she had said. 'Country people may not be loquacious, but they are more than capable of putting two and two together. Hamid has been sufficiently in the public eye already over the business of the man-trap. There is no reason to turn a spotlight on him, and it does not suit my present purpose to do so, particularly as your ticket-collector, from your description of him, appears to be a surly, suspicious man and one with no love for the sheikh and his kind, so keep Hamid's name out of the conversation if you can.'

When I had questioned the man, I was to tackle the booking-clerk. As it turned out, there was nothing to fear from the ticket-collector, for a different man was on duty, a red-cheeked, round-faced boy of about eighteen.

'Does the six o'clock from Ropewalk pull in at the same time every day?' I asked the young countryman. He answered me in a Dorset accent, discernible but removed a long way, I think, from the dialect speech of William Barnes's day, and said:

'It do, sir, but, of course, there's extra trains laid on for Saturdays and Sundays.'

'Sundays?'

'That's right, sir. On account of the golf club, that is. Saturdays it's the football.'

'I see. But otherwise the six o'clock—?'

'If you'd be expecting anybody on the six o'clock *any* day, sir, she run, and she run pretty much to time.'

'Thanks very much. How about the Exeter line?' This was a throwaway question asked for obvious reasons. I did not want the six o'clock train to appear unduly important.

He gave me a detailed reply while I kept half an eye on the booking office to be sure that there would be nobody in the booking hall to hear my questions to the clerk. As soon as opportunity offered I thanked the ticket-collector again and approached the little *guichet*. The clerk, I could tell, remembered me.

'If it's about that there luggage as is directed to the Stag at Strode Hillary, sir,' he said, 'without you've got authority I can't let you remove it.'

'Oh, Lord! Is it still here?' I asked. 'I quite thought it had been collected by this time, but, as I happened to be this way, I thought I'd just make an enquiry.'

'I should be obliged, sir, if you're a friend of the young gentleman, that you'd remind him it's here.'

'No, I'm only his lawyer,' I said, thinking it as well to keep up this fiction. 'I'm on my way to Strode Hillary myself, as a matter of fact. That's why I stopped by to ask about the luggage, although I certainly thought someone would have picked it up by now. I suppose you couldn't—?'

'Sorry, I can't let you have it without the proper slip, sir, glad as I should be to get shut of it. Regulations, you see.'

I put the second of Dame Beatrice's key questions. The first one had been my enquiry to the ticket-collector about the six o'clock train.

'How long has the luggage been in your office, then? I mean, do you charge by the day or the week or what?'

'Last Sunday was a week, sir, the gentleman left it. The entry is in my book, against the number of the ticket I issued. Tickets is what I should say, sir, me having gave him three in all, one for his suitcase, one for his holdall and one for the bag of golf clubs. That's what I reckoned he'd been doing, sir, playing golf, it being Sunday and all.'

I had to press the point, if only to satisfy my own curiosity.

'Are you *sure* it was last Sunday week?'

'Oh, yes, sir. I got the date down in my book. There's been other packages left with me since then, sir, with the date against every one, only *them* packages have all been collected and the slips give in, according to regulations. You ask Mr Okeford, sir, you and him being in the same line of business. He'll tell you same as I do. Sunday gone a week it was. Mr Okeford, he'll tell you. He'd been playing golf, too. He had his bag of clubs with him and, as is usual with him of a Sunday, he shot out of the station to grab a hold of Ben Plush before anybody else could bespeak Ben's taxi.'

Well, I had performed Dame Beatrice's errand and had

collected some information on my own account. I had taken
too much for granted, it seemed. I doubted whether Dame
Beatrice had made the same mistake. Because Hamid had
walked into the man-trap on the Tuesday night and had been
found in the woods by Wally on the Wednesday morning of
my long walk, the walk on which I had visited the burnt-out
shell of Fell Hall, I had assumed all along that Hamid had left
the six o'clock train on the *Tuesday* evening and had been
caught in the trap the same night.

I worked out the various times. I had come to Strode Hillary
on the Sunday, a week and a half ago. On the Monday, Innes
and Mary had taken me to Paulet Marquise church and to
look at the outside of the beautiful manor house of Courtleigh
Purton. On the Tuesday I had paid my visit to Aries St. Peter
church and for the first time I had seen Lower Gushbrook and
its punt. On that day, too, we had been told about the shot
which went through Winters's hat.

On the Wednesday I had taken my walk and Wally had
rescued Hamid ... yes, that was the tally. I had got it all
straight in my mind. Besides, Okeford and his golf clubs surely
clinched matters. It was on a Sunday and not, as I had fondly
concluded, on a Tuesday, that Hamid had left his luggage at
the station. Moreover, it was directed to the Stag and not to
his father's place. That, surely, was a very odd thing.

'Wheels within wheels,' I thought and, hoping by taking
thought while I was alone and undisturbed to find some
solutions to the problems which my visit to the railway station
appeared to be posing, I drove a very long way round to get
back to Strode Hillary. This involved passing the entrance
to the Bourne Farley woods. The entrance to them was
open and there was no sign of the policeman, so I took it for
granted that the sheikh's own guards had also been with-
drawn.

We had had a very late lunch. What with this, my visit to
the station and my long drive home, I was not surprised to find
that the others had not waited tea for me.

'Hurry up, if you want a cup, Mike,' said Mary. 'We're due
at Lord Maumbury's for cocktails and it's a twenty-mile
drive.'

While she was upstairs to get ready for the dinner party, Dame Beatrice and I had a word with Innes.

'Of course,' she said, 'there may be nothing of significance in or about the punt, but an investigation seemed called for.'

'What about the cinders and so forth?' I asked.

'Yes, indeed, what about them?' she said. 'I am under the impression that they were put there for a definite purpose. Somebody who is afraid to bring himself to public notice chose this way to direct attention to the punt, I think.'

'Guilty conscience?' asked Innes.

'Possibly, but more likely one who fears reprisals if he became known as an informer.'

'It sounds more like an American gangster film than life in rural Dorset!' he said.

'Life imitates art, or so we are told.'

'Would you call gangster films art?'

'Perhaps I should ask for notice of that question,' said Dame Beatrice.

While Innes was in the bathroom, I got another word with Dame Beatrice.

'Ah,' she said, when I produced the evidence that Hamid had returned on the Sunday and not on the following Tuesday, 'the plot thickens, Mr Michael, does it not?'

'Strange that Hamid didn't go straight home,' I said. 'It means he must have parked himself somewhere on Sunday night, all day Monday and most of Tuesday. I wonder why? And I wonder who collected all those cinders and things and dumped them on to the punt?'

'As I have said, it must have been somebody who wanted to draw attention to the punt,' she replied, 'and dared not do so openly.' At this point Innes shouted from upstairs that the bathroom was at my disposal, so, a trifle pressed for time, I had no chance to continue the conversation by asking her for more information. However, I chewed over her remarks all the way to Lord Maumbury's house.

CHAPTER 9

EFFIE WINTERS

Even after Lord Maumbury's dinner party – a dull affair with uninspired food and the kind of wine which the vintners tactfully describe as 'suitable for everyday drinking' – there was no suggestion or even veiled hint from Innes and Mary that I should take myself back to London. Rather was it assumed by all three of the others, herself ironically included, that I had become escort, errand-boy and general dogsbody to Dame Beatrice.

While we had been dining out she had been on three errands. I let her have a further and fuller account of what had been said at the station, and she told us of how she had spent her evening.

Hallicks had telephoned soon after we left and said that if she was ready to go to the hospital he would come along immediately and pick her up. This had been done and he had remained outside the private room in which Hamid had been accommodated while she went to the bedside to talk to the boy.

'I told Hamid,' she said to us, 'that I had been in touch with his college.'

' "And they told you that I had not shown up to begin the new term," he said. "What of it? I am tired of College life. I have no interest in obtaining qualifications. I do not need them. My father will keep me and give me money – a great deal of money – while he is alive, and a great deal more will come to me when he dies. It is the custom in our family for all the sons to share the father's wealth. It is not as in England, where the eldest son takes all."

' "Well, not quite all," I said, "but yours seems the better custom." I then asked him what he had been doing on the

Sunday night and all day on the Monday and Tuesday of last week, and that I wondered how he had come to walk into the man-trap. He had received me politely enough, although I detected hostility behind the very smooth façade, and when I entered the room it had been to find a sulkily handsome boy being fussed over by two nurses and enjoying it, but at these questions about his movements his demeanour changed. He raised himself as much as he could and his lips curled back to show his teeth. He said: "I do not answer *women's* questions. Please go away."

'There was no point in my staying. The last thing I intended was to upset him. Besides, I had got the reaction I wanted.'

'I shouldn't have thought you got anything at all,' said Mary.

'Oh, yes, she did,' said Innes. 'We've sometimes had the same sort of reaction in court. As soon as you approach delicate ground the prisoner – perhaps I should say the defendant – soon lets you know it, usually by maintaining a truculent silence which, of course, speaks louder than words.'

'So young Hamid spent Sunday night, all day Monday and until after dark (we think) on Tuesday of last week in a place or in a manner he wasn't willing to discuss,' said Mary. 'Of course, it may just have been that he *meant* he didn't like being questioned by a woman. He is a Moslem and they are brought up to be male chauvinist pigs.'

'Oh, hush! You must not mention those unclean animals in the same breath as the word "Moslem".' said Innes. 'If the Jews and the Arabs ever *really* make common cause, it will be through a common detestation of bacon, and that will include those of us who eat it.'

'You must not talk of a detestation of bacon in front of Dame Beatrice,' retorted Mary. 'She has a favourite nephew who keeps a pig farm. Anyway, do let her finish what she has to say.'

'Superintendent Hallicks then took me to Mr Okeford's house,' said Dame Beatrice. 'Apart from his reputed habit of being first off the mark in pursuit of taxicabs, he seemed an amiable enough man. He agreed at once with Mr Michael's findings. He is a regular Sunday passenger on the six o'clock train from Ropewalk. Golf is his only recreation and he plays always on Sundays. He does not use his car because the car park at the golf club becomes so congested on Sundays that he is afraid of getting his car bumped into and damaged.'

'Martha Lorne told me that he is such a careful man when it comes to giving tips that Plush has threatened to run him over one of these days and wait for a more generous fare,' said Mary.

'I don't see Plush as a murderer,' said Innes.

'Dear me!' said Dame Beatrice. 'I wonder whether he is a gardener as well as a taxi-driver?'

I caught her eye. She nodded.

'Good Lord!' I said. 'So you were right!'

'Thanks to you, my dear Mr Michael. I was interested in your assertion that the wild plants on the humus in the punt had been changed, and yesterday, when we saw the coal-dust and other débris, I felt sure that it clinched matters. It was either a bad mistake on somebody's part, or else it was a warning from a person who had some reason for not going to the police with his suspicions, but who wanted to give a plain signal that something was very wrong.'

'Will someone spell this out?' said Innes.

'Certainly,' replied Dame Beatrice. 'My third visit was to Miss Effie Winters and here, although I can well understand his motive, Superintendent Hallicks allowed me to go into the house and talk to her before he had told me of the result of his excavation of the contents of the punt.'

'Hadn't you asked him about that?' I enquired.

'No. It was police business and I had left it in their hands. What they had found in the punt did not concern me, although I knew what it was.'

'You knew?'

'Certainly. Had they found nothing but what they might have expected to find, he would have told me before I spoke to Miss Winters. As he did not refer to the punt at all, I knew what to think. His excuse, when I challenged him later, was that the body they found would have to be identified. It was a specious excuse, but, of course, I accepted it.'

'You mean Winters's body had been buried in that water-logged punt?' asked Innes. 'So he didn't simply disappear. He died.'

'Murdered.'

'Shot?'

'Stabbed in the back, or so the police surgeon says.'

'Good God! But why?'

'That is what Superintendent Hallicks needs to find out.'

'So when you saw Effie Winters you knew her brother was dead, but you couldn't tell her?'

'I had no official information that her brother was dead and, in any case, it was not my place or my responsibility to tell her what had happened to him.'

'You must have felt pretty awful,' said Mary, 'guessing – well, I suppose, *knowing* – it all, and yet not being able to break the news to her.'

'Well, to speak with some degree of pharisaic hedonism, I saved her at least two days of knowing that a murderer had put an end to her brother's life. It will take at least that much time to get a full medical report and to clean up the body (to put it crudely) sufficiently to make Miss Winters's formal identification of it as little distressing as possible under such very unfortunate circumstances. Naturally she will be upset and distressed when the news is broken to her, but I think we shall find that this derives less from personal and private grief over the loss of her brother and the manner of his ending, than from the unpleasant publicity for herself.'

'You sound cynical and cold-blooded,' said Mary.

'Are you prepared to tell us about the interview?' asked Innes. 'If so, perhaps I had better withdraw. The case will go to the coroner and then, most likely, it will come to us, so that we can make a committal charge. In that case, the less I know beforehand the better.'

'The coroner will see to it that his jury brings in a verdict of murder by person or persons unknown, won't he?' I asked. 'There can't be a hearing before the magistrates until the police have made an arrest, and after that the hearing will be nothing but a formality. The accused is bound to be sent for trial. What you know at this juncture can't possibly affect the issue.'

However, he retained his scruples and went out of the room while Dame Beatrice told us how the interview with Effie Winters had gone. I had never encountered Effie, of course, but my knowledge of Dame Beatrice, so far as it went, predisposed me to believe that her description of Winters's sister and her estimate of her were as near complete accuracy as makes no matter.

As it had been already getting towards dusk when Dame Beatrice knocked, Effie prudently called out to ask who was there before she answered the door. Reassured (I imagine) by Dame Beatrice's beautiful voice and, no doubt, relieved that the caller was a woman, Effie opened up and apologised for her previous hesitation.

'When you're on your own you need to be careful these days,' she said. 'One hears such dreadful things.'

'I should hardly have thought they applied to Strode Hillary,' said Dame Beatrice, making a calculated opening move. She was invited into a small sitting-room where a deep armchair was flanked by what she diagnosed as a cocktail cabinet. On the opposite side of the fireplace was a smaller, less luxurious armchair, and to the right of this a piece of furniture which used to be called a chiffonier. Its cupboard door was half open to disclose an untidy pile of women's magazines, and on its sideboard top were a few pieces of Victorian china, remnants, perhaps, from a childhood home in which they had been ancestral relics once treasured by some great-grand-mother.

'Do take Skiddy's chair,' said Effie. 'You say you're working with the police?'

'Yes, indeed. My card may assure you of my official standing.'

Effie, a woman who (Dame Beatrice said) looked as though she kept and cherished aspidistras, although there were none of these in the sitting-room, took the card by its extreme corner and even then only between over-long finger and thumbnail and said, as she laid it on the arm of her chair:

'All right, if you want to ask me any questions. All the same, though, anybody can get a card printed, can't they?'

'It would be a criminal act to reproduce this one unlawfully. Such a reproduction could only be made for criminal purposes, I think.'

'Do the police think Skiddy is a criminal?'

'Not so far as I know. What makes you ask?'

'He's paid all his debts. They were a millstone round his neck, and now they've all melted away.'

'A thing millstones are disinclined to do. How do you know that the debts are cleared? I was told, on whose authority I know not, that certain monies were to accrue to your brother within a year or two. I was told that he would be able to extricate himself from his difficulties when some insurance policies fell due for realisation. I take it that that is what happened.'

(This information, I surmised, could only have come to Dame Beatrice from Okeford, but I asked no questions.)

She went on to tell us that a flush came into Effie's ordinarily pale face and she laughed on a high, slightly hysterical note.

'Catch Skiddy using his *own* money to pay his debts!' she said. 'Anyway, the policies hadn't matured.'

'Skiddy? An unusual nickname.'

'Not really. He was christened Skiddaw because my father and mother had spent a holiday in the Lake District the year before he was born and they thought the name went well with Winters. Of course the family shortened the name to Skiddy and that's what he's been ever since – Skiddy by name and skiddy by nature – and if you want to know what I think, he's skidded once and for all. The police know he was involved in those local robberies. They told me so, and asked me all sorts of questions.'

'But Superintendent Hallicks decided, I think, that there was nothing useful that you could tell him.'

'That being so, what do you want of me? I can't tell you anything I didn't tell him. I told him all I know, and that's little enough, goodness knows! When you said just now that dreadful things couldn't happen in Strode Hillary, don't you know that Skiddy got a bullet that might have killed him? Yes, and what about the poor boy who got caught in that dreadful man-trap? Yes, and that other boy who tried to drown himself in Strode Water, only Farmer Breedy got to him in time and pulled him out and gave him a hiding for being such a young fool.'

'I don't think Superintendent Hallicks knows about that. When did it happen?'

'Last Wednesday week. No reason why the police *should* know anything about it.'

'Is it known why the youth wished to drown?'

'Something to do with a girl, I expect. It usually is, when they go in for suicide at that age.'

'What is the young man's name?'

'Breedy, same as his father's. That's why Amos Breedy felt free to give him a drubbing, I suppose.'

'I see. Do you know Farmer Breedy well?'

'Only through Skiddy. They had dealings together at one time, but Skiddy was on the fiddle, as they call it, and Breedy gave up being partners with him. If it had been anybody but Skiddy trying to do the negotiations, I think the Arab gentleman would have got Long Fallow, but when Breedy heard that Skiddy was behind the deal he washed his hands of it and said he wouldn't sell for any price, however fancy, if Skiddy was to get his cut of it.'

'So your brother discussed his business interests with you.'

'That would be a rare laugh!'

'Where is Long Fallow?'

'Borders on the Bourne Farley property and makes a kind of strip between the Bourne Farley home farm and the river.'

'The river in which young Breedy tried to drown himself?'

'Oh, no. The proper river, the Meddle. Seems the Arab gentleman's sons, the schoolboys that only come home for the holidays, like a bit of fishing. If their father could get Long Fallow the boys could get access, you see, and even do a bit of swimming, I suppose.'

'Surely the sheikh has a heated outdoor pool? I thought all wealthy men had one nowadays.'

'Not much fun for schoolboys. Besides, seems it was the

fishing mostly they wanted. It's preserved along the Meddle, you see. Well, Breedy made the excuse that Long Fallow was agricultural and told the sheikh the land must be kept under crops, but Okeford could get round that one if he'd a mind to, because, until the war, Long Fallow used to be pasture. It's only for building land it can't be sold, I reckon. It was just to spite Skiddy he wouldn't sell.'

'And Mr Okeford refused to handle the transaction?'

'He might have been willing to handle it if there had been the slightest sign that Breedy would sell, but there wasn't. Breedy is a very stubborn man.'

'I heard that there was an incident with a car which your brother was driving.'

'He ran into Breedy's lorry. That wasn't Skiddy's fault. The brakes had been tampered with. They never found out who did it, but although Skiddy wasn't disqualified, it shook his nerve and he never drove a car again.'

'I heard that he was the only person who escaped injury.'

'That's the way the devil takes care of his own. He was in the wrong in so far he knew the car was an old crock and only tinkered up. He should have tested the brakes before starting. Some of the hills round here are one in six and there's the Dun that's one in five.'

'Do the injured men bear your brother any ill-will?'

'Pub threats, I expect, that's all. They took a chance and got a lift and didn't really have any right to complain. One of them couldn't complain, anyway, because he was killed. His wife talked of a prosecution but she must have dropped it, because it never came to anything. Skiddy went in fear of Rigg Halstock, though. He always said Rigg would get back at him some day.'

'But that does not explain why your brother is missing, does it?'

'I was worried at first when Skiddy didn't come home, but when Burrows split on him about the burglaries I could understand well enough. Skiddy, like I told you, suddenly had plenty of money—'

'From the proceeds of the burglaries?'

'Could hardly be that. The police found the stuff at Fell
Hall. Skiddy and Burrows didn't have time to sell it.'

'Then where did the money come from?'

'I don't have any idea. It was some fiddle Skiddy had on,
only he always called them "schemes". Most of them didn't
come off because he wasn't nearly as clever as he thought he
was, but something must have come right for him and it
couldn't have been the burglaries.'

'Perhaps he had previous thefts to his discredit and had
realised on those.'

'It could be, I suppose. If so, I do hope nothing comes out.
I've always prided myself. It *could* be that, I suppose.'

'But she seemed so doubtful,' said Dame Beatrice, telling us
the story, 'that I deduced that her brother's achievement of
affluence had been sudden and surprising. However, one thing
is certain: she may have been worried when he disappeared,
but I doubt whether she will grieve for him unduly when she
learns that he is dead. There was little love lost between them,
I imagine.'

'Why was she so upset when he disappeared, then?' I asked.

'Oh yes! She hoped that nothing would come out.'

'Poor Effie!' said Mary, with genuine sympathy. 'She's a
member of the W.I. and I believe she belongs to the Towns-
women's Guild in Ropewalk, but I don't really know her.
Anyway, we're holding up Dame Beatrice's story.'

'I have nothing more to tell. Whatever her brother's
peccadilloes, I do not think Miss Winters took any part in
them or even knew exactly what they were,' said Dame
Beatrice. 'So far as the flow to Winters of unexpected wealth
was concerned, I hinted at blackmail, but she did not appear
to understand my carefully veiled suggestions and I can
usually tell when a patient is attempting to hoodwink me. She
lied on one count, I think. Winters paid his own debts, unless
she paid them knowing that he was dead.'

'Well, if you have no more to tell us, I'll tell Innes to come
back and pour us all a nightcap,' said Mary.

'So Winters – I suppose there's no doubt in Hallicks's mind
that it *is* Winters – has been murdered, and the shot through
his hat was no accident,' I said. 'I wonder what his sister's

public reaction will be when she is told what has happened?'

'Shock, but not grief, I fancy,' said Dame Beatrice. 'I was left with a positive feeling not only that she guesses what has happened, but also that she may be very glad to be rid of him.'

'That is probably true. She may not grieve for him, but she's in for a great deal of unpleasantness, isn't she? First of all, however she feels about her brother, she is bound to have to face a great deal of publicity.'

'And to have to identify the body! I think that's quite the beastliest experience,' said Mary, 'and she will have to give evidence before the coroner, won't she?'

'And probably at the trial, if the police catch the murderer,' I remarked. 'My word, though!' I visualised the scene. 'I don't envy the police who had to dig the body out of that punt! I'm very glad somebody strewed all that coal-dust and rubbish. I should have hated my little trowel to have come upon something nasty, and I suppose it would have done.'

'It would not have done so,' Dame Beatrice assured me. 'As soon as we had come upon anything suspicious, however slight, I should have called a halt to our operations and proceeded (as, in fact, we did proceed) to leave everything to Superintendent Hallicks and his men.'

'But what made you think of the punt as a receptacle for a dead body?' I asked. 'You didn't know about the cinders and grit and stuff when we went along with our trowels.'

'Anything out of the ordinary interests me,' she said, 'and as several people must have had unfriendly feelings towards Winters, his disappearance could be accounted for in one of two ways. Either he had fled the neighbourhood or he was dead. The shot through his hat disposed me to think that the second assumption could well be the right one.'

'Effie took long enough to report his disappearance,' said Innes. 'It was as long ago as last Friday when you noticed the different plants.'

'We are assuming that the murderer tidied up the punt,' said Dame Beatrice, 'but, of course, there could be another explanation.'

It turned out, however, that Effie's delay in informing the

police of her brother's disappearance could be accounted for
without helping to bridge the time-gap. Our information
came, as usual, from Martha Lorne. She met Mary in the
town and handed out the facts and the rumours. Mary
returned with these.

'Hallicks is gunning for poor Effie Winters,' she said.
'Apparently Winters and Effie had a long and bitter quarrel
on the Tuesday evening.'

'After the bullet went through his hat?' asked Innes.

'Yes. I suppose that had unnerved him and he took it out on
his sister. The neighbours heard the quarrel and the noise of
furniture being thrown about and crockery smashed, and
the householder next door told Hallicks that his wife became
so much alarmed that he stepped over the front railings
and hammered on the front door to remonstrate with
Winters. Nobody answered the door, but the hint seems to
have been taken and the shouting and all the sounds of
violence ceased. An hour later Effie was seen by another
neighbour walking down the street carrying a small suitcase.'

This and the rest of the story came out in the local paper.
Effie had gone to friends in Yeovil and had stayed with them
from the Tuesday night until the Friday evening. When she
found that her brother was not at home and did not show
up that night, she was not alarmed. She also allowed Saturday to pass, supposing that he was staying with a woman. On Sunday there was still no sign of him and she
became worried, and when on Monday he was still missing and an examination of his bedroom showed that he
had not taken so much as a change of underclothing
with him, she went to the police. At least, that was the
story.

The next news was startling and bizarre. The possible time
and day of Winters's death was still not known, according to
Hallicks, who had spoken to Innes, but it could have been as
early as the Tuesday night of the quarrel. The body had been
put in cold storage, probably in a large deep freeze, the
pathologist thought. Even when the police dug it out of the
punt it had not entirely thawed out.

'Thank goodness a turkey is about the largest item our fridge will take,' said Innes. 'But, you know, Mike, even if Effie did the murder, she must have had help with the burial. By the way, my talk with Hallicks about the body was in the strictest confidence and very little of what he told me will come out at the inquest.'

CHAPTER 10

FARMER BREEDY

'Well, once the news about the body in the punt gets around, I don't envy the village of Lower Gushbrook. It will be absolutely swarming with newspapermen,' said Innes, later. 'The local reporters will have the time of their lives and the whole thing is sufficiently out of the ordinary to attract the big dailies, I shouldn't wonder. I think we'll keep away from Lower Gushbrook for a bit. What do you think, Dame Beatrice?'

'Dame Beatrice will have to rely on the discretion of the police,' said Mary, 'and so shall we, too, because if the papers get to know that she discovered where the body was buried we shall have them round here, so avoiding Lower Gushbrook won't be any help about that.'

'I did not discover where the body was buried. That piece of deduction must be credited to Mr Michael,' said Dame Beatrice. 'I should never have thought twice about the submerged punt but for his accurate observation and retentive memory.'

I looked at Mary. She smiled.

'There are things one does remember and things one doesn't,' I said. 'It depends upon luck and the circumstances. If I had been with Innes, for example, I doubt whether I should have noticed the plants the first time and, that being the case, I should not have realised, when I looked at the punt the second time, that the plants had been changed.'

'Well, I think I'll tip the wink to Hallicks that a word with Chettle and Batcombe might be not a bad idea,' said Innes.

'I myself would like a word with Farmer Breedy before I see the sheikh's son again,' said Dame Beatrice. Innes looked surprised.

'Breedy?' he said. 'But you don't suspect him of knowing anything about the murder, do you?'

'I want to know why his son attempted to commit suicide and I want to be sure that young Breedy and not young Hamid was on the wooden bridge when Mr Michael took his walk that morning.'

'Hamid?' I said, surprised in my turn.

'You mentioned a swarthy young man, or so Innes informed me. Hamid is swarthy; Hamid was caught in the mantrap; Hamid does not want to talk to me; and somebody put a knife in Winters's back. I am interested in these facts, that is all.'

'If you go to see Breedy, either Mike or I will go with you,' said Innes. 'Breedy is an honest sort of chap, but he can be abusive or even violent.'

'You said much the same thing about the youths I interviewed,' said Dame Beatrice, 'but they were meekness itself.'

'There is a very strong belief in witchcraft around these parts,' said Innes, grinning. 'You probably cast a spell on them – or they thought you did or could.'

'I should hardly have thought the younger generation would have been so misled.'

'I'd like to know what happened to that doll from the museum,' said Mary. 'Aren't dolls tied up with some forms of witchcraft?'

We soon knew what had happened to the doll. The police had found it when they dug up Winters's body. It had been tied face-downwards across his chest and when they examined it they found a darning-needle stuck through it.

Dame Beatrice made no objection to my escorting her to Breedy's farm. She could do with a witness, she said. I warned her about Breedy's Alsatians, but the warning left her unperturbed. We went in my car, for the farm had an entrance from the hilly road which skirted the church, a road I had avoided when I took my walk.

The only dog about the place, when we approached the front door of the farmhouse, was a rough-coated retriever which I thought I recognised. He was lying across the doorstep as though on guard. I gave him my fingers to smell, upon which he got up and wagged his tail, so I stepped forward and rang the bell. A young girl, aged about seventeen, I thought, opened the door and looked at Dame Beatrice, who produced one of her useful official cards.

The girl read it and asked us in and, as we entered, a man's voice shouted a question from somewhere upstairs.

'You better come down, Gaffer,' the girl called back. 'Company to see you, and put your jacket on. There's a lady present.'

An elderly, but not an old, man came down the stairs. He held on to the banisters and was limping badly. As he reached the foot of the stairs the girl put a stout walking-stick into his hand. He looked us over, grunted and then said, 'This way,' and led us down the passage to a room which appeared to be the farmhouse parlour.

Here he waved Dame Beatrice to an old-fashioned wooden armchair with an upholstered seat and then he limped across to it and thrust a cushion behind her spare, upright back. He seated himself opposite her and left me to fend for myself, so I took an upright chair at the table and laid out my notepaper and ballpoint. He grunted again at this and said, with ferocious humour,

'Taken down in writing and given in evidence, then?'

'Our intentions are honourable,' said Dame Beatrice. 'You will be asked to sign Mr Michael's notes when he has transcribed his shorthand. We would like you to be certain that what he says you have said is simply that and nothing more or less.'

'Fair enough,' he said. 'I'm a cautious man. I don't say much and I've a good memory for what I've said.'

'And have Yorkshire forebears, although you yourself were born here in Dorset.' She obviously surprised him by this remark and he asked,

'How the devil do you know ours was a Yorkshire family?'

'By your manners and by your blue eyes. Those eyes could only come from Yorkshire stock. This fact was brought to my notice years ago at a cocktail party by a drunken painter of seascapes.'

The clamped muscles around Farmer Breedy's obstinate mouth relaxed and he almost smiled.

'Well, compliments and the reverse aside,' he said, 'what might you want with me?'

'All that you know about man-traps and Mr Winters and dolls and Mr Hamid Aziz and, most of all, what you know about the fatal accident to a Mr Lorne, when the car in which he was a passenger collided with your lorry some months ago.'

'Right.' He looked across at me. 'Got all that down, young fellow?'

'Yes, Mr Breedy, but you flatter me. I am turned forty years old. How did you damage your foot? You were spry enough the other day when I met you and your dog.'

'Put a fork through it, that's what.'

'I knew I had left out something,' said Dame Beatrice. 'If it will not provoke a burst of profanity or even ordinary invective, may I ask why your son contemplated suicide on the morning you met Mr Michael?'

The farmer stared at her, but not, I thought, belligerently. He cleared his throat, in fact, rather apologetically before he answered. Then he said,

'Young Bob was afraid to tell me what had happened. Got a girl into trouble and said he couldn't afford to marry. Only one way out of that. Old-fashioned but sensible. I made him put up the banns and they'll be married come harvest. Cost me a packet to soften up her father, him being Okeford, the lawyer fellow, and not wanting my boy for a son-in-law, thinking his girl could do better when once she'd got rid of the baby.'

'How badly did you want Winters killed?'

He stared again.

'What's happened to him?' he asked. 'You mean he's dead?'

'His body, stabbed in the back, has been found at Lower Gushbrook,' said Dame Beatrice, looking at him as I have been told a stoat looks at a rabbit or a snake looks at a bird. Breedy shook his head and continued to stare at her. 'Well?' she said. 'You threatened him, did you not?'

'My boy's my boy. He may be a fool and lascivious with it, but he's still my boy.'

'Even the Devil looks after his own, which, considering what scoundrels his own are, is to his credit, I think,' said Dame Beatrice.

'You're muddling up my mind, mistress. What do you want
me to tell you?'

'Who killed Winters, of course.'

'Nay, if I knew that, I'd shake his bloody hand.'

'As Marcus Antonius did with Caesar's murderers. Strange,
you know, that when we speak of Caesar we are always
understood to refer to Julius, yet there were many Caesars.
Why should that one appear to have unique right to the title?
Have you ever wondered why, Mr Breedy?'

The farmer looked appealingly at me, but all I could do was
to look commiseratingly back at him. He sighed and said,

'What's all this about, anyway?'

'Murder,' said Dame Beatrice briskly, 'as I thought we were
agreed. You say you do not know who murdered Winters.
From what I hear and from what I deduce from what I hear,
there could be several suspects. Let us leave the subject and
talk about man-traps.'

'One thing I know about them. If things were taken out of
the museum, there is only one lad that took 'em, and that's
young Peter Chettle. Nobody else would have had the
opportunity.'

'Would he have set the man-trap after he had stolen it?'

'Could have done, I reckon. He's wicked enough.'

'What about dolls?'

'Can't think why he should have taken a doll. Toys for little
girls, they be. Still, young Chettle's daffy.'

'The doll was found buried with Winters's body.'

'That's witchcraft, then. Ay, I've heard of that.'

'Who in this neighbourhood, apart from yourself, is likely to
have heard that dolls are connected with black magic?'

'You, for one,' said Breedy, with, to my surprise, a chuckle.
'Oh, well, it would likely be a woman, anyway. Women go for
old wives' tales, don't 'em? That Mrs Lorne, now, always
busybodying about. I wouldn't be surprised if she knew
something of dolls with pins stuck in 'em. When her husband
was killed she went very strange for a bit until the Reverend
took her to task and talked her out of it. Had it in for me
properly, she did. Blamed my lorry for Lorne's death. Strange,
that.'

I thought that, little as I knew of her, there certainly seemed nothing strange about Martha Lorne except, of course, the very strange fact that she had never mentioned the death of her husband to Innes and Mary. However, I realised that Dame Beatrice had now reached the subject she really wanted Breedy to talk about. She caught my eye and nodded to me to apply myself to my shorthand.

'Yes, Mrs Lorne went very strange for a time,' repeated Breedy. 'Shut herself away and burnt candles instead of using the electric light, and at nights, the neighbours said, she used to go down to the little stream that flows past the houses at that end of the town before it diverts away across the meadow, and she would step into it with her shoes on and say her prayers standing up in it and then she would laugh and laugh. Got folk real worried, she did, and there was talk of calling in the doctors and having her put away before she could do harm to herself, but the Reverend was against it. He said he would have a try first, because she had had a very bad shock with her husband getting killed so providential, and that would account for her acting daffy.'

'How do you mean? Providential? Why?' asked Dame Beatrice. 'I thought you said she was angry about his death.'

'In debt for miles around, Mrs Lorne were, but the insurances she'd taken out on Lorne paid up very handsome and cleared up everything. She paid every penny that was owing, and got shut of him into the bargain.'

'It was not a happy marriage?'

'God knows. There was talk about somebody tampering with the brakes of the car, but nothing came of it.'

'Whose car was it?'

'Lorne's own car.'

'But Winters was driving it, I understand. Why was that?'

'On account Lorne was trying to flog it to him.'

'And the accident took place on your land?'

'Not in hell it didn't! My lorry was parked halfway down Napper Hill with a load of gravel I'd ordered for a front path me and my son were going to put down when we had time. The car came belting down the hill, which has a nasty bend in it. The horn was blaring all the time, so the driver, Winters, must have known the brakes were faulty. Even so, I reckon he could have saved an accident if he'd kept his head, but he didn't. Whether the car got right out of his control, or whether he had some daffy idea as it was better to smash into my lorry than to go on and risk the steepest part of the hill, I don't know. He took the lorry kind of sideways on. Lorne, who was sitting next Winters, was killed outright, being on the side next the lorry, and Halstock and his boy were hurt pretty serious, them being at the back, which took a lot of the impact as the car slewed round.'

'Were you with your lorry?'

'No. One of my chaps was in charge of it. He was in the pub. That's why the lorry was parked where it was. He heard the row Winters's horn was making, but by the time he got outside the damage was done.'

'Was your lorry parked in such a way as to cause a hazard, do you think?'

'No, of course it wasn't. It was right off the road in the forecourt of the pub. It was damaged, of course, by the impact.'

'How much truth was there in the rumour that the brakes of the car had been tampered with?'

'The car was too badly smashed up for anybody to be able to swear to that. It was Winters's story and Lorne couldn't support it or otherwise, being dead; nor could Martha, her being away on a visit when the crash happened.'

'I don't suppose the other two passengers knew much about it,' I said.

'Both knocked unconscious,' he agreed, 'and come to only to find themselves in hospital.'

'Did Halstock senior ever utter any threats?' Dame Beatrice asked.

'There was a court case, as I say, and that's all I know. My chap had to attend, but him and my lorry were completely exonerated and anyway he got outside too late for his statement to be any help, so they accepted Winters's story about faulty brakes.'

'Was young Walter Halstock called upon to give evidence?'

'No. He and his dad were still in hospital. There was only

Winters to speak to what happened, so they had to take his word for it about the brakes.'

'How did Halstock and his son come to be in the car? Were they also possible customers for it?'

'Not they. No, it was just that they were at Lorne's place and Winters said Lorne told him to give them a lift.'

'Were you in court to hear the evidence?'

'Yes, and at the inquest, too. My chap with the lorry wanted me to be there.'

'But he must have known that no blame could be attached to him if the lorry was stationary and he was inside the public house when the crash occurred.'

'Been fined once before for drunken driving and it made him nervous as he had to allow he was in a pub, you see.'

'I wonder you kept him on in your employment after he had been fined for drunken driving.'

'Oh, it wasn't one of my vehicles he was driving. Poor chap had just lost his wife, so I reckon he was entitled to drown his sorrows. I spoke up for him as best I could.'

'And paid the fine,' said Dame Beatrice.

'What if I did? He had enough expense burying his good lady. Funerals don't come cheap.'

'Nor the funeral bakemeats after the interment. Do you possess a deep freeze, Mr. Breedy?'

Breedy stared at her again.

'Only for my own use,' he said. 'Why?'

'The thought of funeral bakemeats put the thought into my head, I suppose.'

'Women's heads be always inside the larder,' said the farmer, accepting this explanation. 'Yes, I have a deep freeze. Got half a pig and a leg of beef in it and half-a-dozen fowls and a duck or two.'

'There cannot be many people in these parts with this useful receptacle, I fancy.'

'Other farmers maybe, and the big houses and the hotel. You got one?'

'No. I have an ordinary refrigerator, that is all. My household is small.'

'Oh, ah.' He looked at her card which he had placed on the

arm of his chair. 'Home Office, eh? What's your game in these parts, then?'

'I am often called in when cases of murder appear to hinge on the mental state of a suspect.'

'You don't need to worry about young Wally Halstock. Harmless as a baby.'

'And his father?'

'Took the loss of his arm very hard, as who wouldn't? I don't see him accepting any more lifts in cars.'

'I hear he used to be Lord Maumbury's gardener.'

'Ah, that's right.'

'How about Mrs Lorne? Did she know her husband was trying to sell the car to Winters?'

'I couldn't say. At the inquest she told the coroner she had been away visiting her mother.'

'And Effie Winters was away from home at what may well have been the day of her brother's death, and in both cases insurance policies appear to have been involved. These coincidences are very strange and may even be significant,' said Dame Beatrice. Breedy looked as though he was about to make a remark, but apparently he changed his mind, for all he did was to spit into the open fire and then lean back in his chair. Dame Beatrice, who had paused to give him a chance to speak, continued: 'How did the Halstocks come to be in the car?'

'Told you they were given a lift.'

'Were they on the road, walking , I mean?'

'He said not. He said they were outside Lorne's place. He said if they'd been on the road and thumbed a lift he'd have found out the brakes were faulty before the car was on that downhill gradient, and he could have pulled up quietly and there'd have been much less chance of an accident.'

'And if Lorne had been driving the car the chances are that he would have been safe and Winters killed,' I said, when we were on our way home. 'Do you think Lorne was the intended victim? It doesn't look as though anybody could have known that the Halstocks would also be in the car. Mind you, if the brakes *had* been tampered with, the likeliest person to have done it, because she would have had the best opportunity, is Martha Lorne herself, before she went on her visit.'

'Would a woman know enough about cars to put the brakes wrong?' asked Mary, when we reported our interview.

Dame Beatrice said: 'Breedy contradicted himself in the strangest way about Mrs Lorne. I am beginning to think that what with the incident of the man-trap and now Winters's murder, it may be necessary to study whatever evidence there is of how that car crash occurred. If young Hamid Aziz had not been struck on the head while, presumably, he was unconscious as a result of shock or pain, I might take a very different view of the man-trap affair, but—'

'Yes, who would have done a dastardly thing like that to an already wounded and suffering man?' said Mary.

'Somebody who thought Hamid would die from the blow on the head,' said Dame Beatrice.

'Well, you'll have a good choice of suspects lined up for this murder if you think there is a connection between that and the car crash,' said Innes, 'won't you?'

'It is the several months of time-lag which pose the mystery so far as a possible connection is concerned,' she replied.

'Well, yes, but country minds, as I have often thought, work slowly over some matters. They dwell on things and brood and only gradually come to conclusions. If this murder had been committed in a large town I would agree with you, but in this particular case I don't think the time-lag is of any great importance,' I said.

'I wonder where the murder actually took place?' said Innes.

'In Winters's own home, most likely,' I suggested. 'His death seems to have done his sister quite a bit of good.'

'Yes. She benefited from her brother's insurance policies and Mrs Lorne benefited from those of her husband,' said Dame Beatrice, 'and, as we have heard, both women have provided themselves with alibis.'

'What beastly stuff money is!' said Mary. Innes smiled and patted the breast pocket where he kept his wallet.

'A nice little sum for the article I wrote the other week,' he said, 'but I won't buy you a present out of it if you'd rather I didn't.'

'Wonder when Breedy stuck that gardening-fork through his foot?' I said.

'Or that pitchfork,' amended Dame Beatrice. 'There are other uses for pitchforks than tossing the hay, if, in fact, hay *is* tossed by pitchfork in this mechanised age.'

'Why do you think it wasn't a gardening-fork? I should have thought it far more likely, as he stuck it through his foot.'

'You may well be right, although farmers are seldom keen gardeners,' she said.

'He may not have been gardening. I only wondered *when* he did it, that's all. The implement itself doesn't matter. The people in these parts seem accident-prone. Hamid gets caught in a man-trap, Breedy gives himself a nasty flesh-wound and Winters gets himself murdered. Only a few months ago, Lorne gets killed, young Halstock gets a serious knock on the head and his father loses an arm.'

'Winters seems to have become pretty flush before he was murdered,' I said, 'and you thought Effie told some lies about whether he himself paid his debts.'

'Yes, indeed,' Dame Beatrice agreed, 'and that fact, coupled with his death by violence, may be very significant.'

'Blackmail?'

'A possibility, I feel. It would be interesting and perhaps important to know exactly where Winters was when he was murdered. The suggestion that it was in his own home would be more likely if that home contained a large deep freeze. No doubt Superintendent Hallicks will be checking the houses which possess this amenity.'

CHAPTER 11

AN INQUEST AND AFTER

To put the matter crudely, I suppose I felt a kind of proprietory interest in Winters's body as it was I who had noticed the plants in the punt, and this caused me to attend the inquest. After all, had it not been for me, Dame Beatrice would never have suspected that the rotting little hulk contained mortal remains, and she had acknowledged this.

The proceedings were held in Ropewalk and the coroner (so Innes, who accompanied Dame Beatrice and me, informed us) was the solicitor, Okeford. From his reputation as a grabber of taxis I expected to see a lantern-jawed ferrety man, but he was blond, bluff and cheerful and for this reason I believe I disliked and distrusted him more than if he had looked the way I had pictured him.

Nothing was dealt with at this preliminary session except evidence of identification (given by Effie Winters who looked, according to the newspapers next day, pale but composed); the medical evidence of a death by stabbing; and a formal request by Hallicks, who came up to speak to us after the proceedings were over, that the police were asking for an adjournment to give them time to pursue their enquiries. This was after the jury had brought in a verdict which could hardly be questioned: wilful murder by person or persons unknown.

I must admit that Okeford made an excellent coroner. His legal training had made him precise and logical, so no time was wasted, neither did he pontificate. He took evidence of identification first. Effie Winters agreed to her name and address (it was the first time I had ever heard Effie as a diminutive of Serafina, and I do not believe it is a usual one), and then she was asked whether she had been shown the body. She was pallid but quite composed and tearless and agreed that she had seen the body.

'Was it one that you recognised?'

'Yes, it was the body of my brother, Skiddaw William Winters.'

'And a very nice job the doctors had done in cleaning him up,' Hallicks confided to us later. 'Nothing distressing for her to see, not even the nasty look he had in life. You'd have said he died really peaceful. That's the beauty of being stabbed in the back, I reckon. He didn't even have time to register horror or pain or anything. There was one item we asked to have suppressed, but it didn't affect the verdict.'

The medical evidence, which included a lot of technical stuff that meant nothing to the layman but sounded important and impressive, had not taken up much of the coroner's time. All I gathered was that the wound – there was only one – had been made with a sharp-pointed weapon, probably double-edged. It would have had an approximate blade length of at least six inches, but a juror who asked whether the weapon could have been of Middle-Eastern origin was smartly slapped down by the coroner.

'That question will not be recorded,' said Okeford. 'All things considered, it is a most improper one and I suggest to any newspaper reporters present that they disregard it. In my opinion it contains a scandalous innuendo which could form a basis for an action for libel if it were ever disseminated in print.'

'All the same,' said Innes, when we were on our way home, 'the chap only voiced what a lot of people are thinking. They would sooner believe that a knife in the back was the work of one of the sheikh's men than that it was a British solution to a problem.'

'The police are still looking for the murder weapon, I suppose,' I said. 'I wonder how much it will tell them when they find it?'

The next thing we heard was that Hallicks had arrested Effie Winters and that she was to appear before the magistrates charged with the murder of her brother.

'Will you be at the hearing?' I asked Innes.

'I'm afraid so, yes,' he answered. 'I can hardly declare an interest and get out of it that way. I didn't even know the woman, except by sight. Even then I knew her only as Winters's sister. I do know, though, that he was so much disliked and distrusted that everybody felt sorry for her. She may have got so tired of living with him that she took the drastic course.'

'Others must be involved,' said Mary. 'Even if she killed Winters, she couldn't have buried him in the punt. That waterlogged soil would be much too heavy for a woman to dig out and put back.'

'Don't you believe it,' said Innes. 'What about our sturdy land-girls during the war? Besides, it's amazing what people can do when they are driven to it. Hallicks is a level-headed, sensible chap. He must have a thundering good case if he's already arrested and charged Effie Winters.'

'Well, the stab in the back and the doll with the darning needle do suggest a woman,' I said, 'and if people were sorry for Effie Winters they must have known that she had a good deal to put up with. There's a motive, isn't there?'

'I don't know so much,' said Mary. 'A sister isn't like a wife. She could have walked out of his house at any time if she didn't like it there.'

'If she had any money or anywhere else to go,' I said.

'Well, she has inherited money, it seems,' said Dame Beatrice. 'No doubt Superintendent Hallicks has given full consideration to that fact. Her brother's insurance policies, which she herself may have taken out, could supply her with an income, no doubt.'

'Yes, the first thing the police look for is a money motive. I think it's so sordid of them,' said Mary. Innes and I laughed and Dame Beatrice said:

'More often than not, money is the motive for murder, and Miss Winters must be suspect on that count and, I suppose, on two others.'

'Two others?' said Mary. 'Oh, you mean the deep freeze, but I shouldn't think Winters had one, you know. What Hallicks ought to look at are the farms. It's a horrible thought that while they were being blessed the body was in one of their kitchens.'

'Oh, no, it wasn't,' I said. 'It was already buried. The plants in the punt prove that.'

'Not necessarily,' said Innes. 'We don't know what plants there were, or if there were any plants at all, under all that coal-dust and rubbish you and Dame Beatrice saw. The changing of the plants could have an entirely innocent explanation. It could have been the work of children, as one of us mentioned. The coal-dust and rubbish may not have been somebody's attempt to draw attention to the punt, but a clumsy way of disguising the fact that the surface of the waterlogged soil had been disturbed again.'

This was a new point of view and not one that I relished. I had been so proud of my powers of observation and my botanical knowledge that it was hard to have them discounted.

'Well, there is one way to find out,' I said, 'and no doubt Hallicks has thought of it. He has only to enquire at the school.'

'Let's check up,' said Innes. 'It isn't that I don't think you have a point, Mike. It's the deep freeze angle that puzzles me. If, as you claim, the murder could have been committed as long ago as the Tuesday night after Winters got the bullet through his hat, why didn't the murderer and his accomplice bury the body on the Wednesday morning? We know they didn't because, if they had, the deep freeze which was supposed to disguise the time of death would have been unnecessary.'

'It did disguise it,' I argued. 'We don't know, and Hallicks doesn't know, on which day or night Winters was murdered. We can only place it within the space of time between the Tuesday when Mary and I saw the original wild plants in position and the Friday (which means dawn on the Friday morning) when I pointed out later to Dame Beatrice that they had been changed.'

'We've had all this out before,' said Mary. 'What I want to get at is Dame Beatrice's second point. The deep freeze I disagree with, unless Effie had access to one and therefore had an accomplice. What is the other, godmamma?'

'Effie Winters's very convenient alibi, I suppose,' said Innes, looking at Dame Beatrice for confirmation. 'It would take a very stupid policeman to find nothing suspicious in the fact

that Effie opted out of Strode Hillary just at the time that her
brother was about to be murdered.'

I pointed out that alibis can usually be checked and that I
had no doubt Hallicks had checked this one and found a
leakage in it.

'She herself went to the police and reported that her brother
was missing,' said Mary. 'Doesn't that let Effie Winters out?'

'That is hardly a valid argument in favour of her innocence,' said Dame Beatrice. 'Even if *she* had not reported his
absence, it could not have been long before others noticed that
her brother was missing. Once it was established that he had
disappeared, rumours would have flown around and her
silence on the matter would soon have aroused suspicion.'

'What was Winters like?' I asked Innes. 'I mean, granted
that a woman could have stabbed him to death with one clean
blow in the right place, and granted that she would have been
strong enough to have dug a hole long enough and deep
enough to bury him, how did she get the body to Lower
Gushbrook? If she did kill Winters, it must have been done in
his own home, surely? – so how did she transport the body?'

'Hallicks must have information which he's keeping to
himself,' said Innes.

He did not keep it to himself for very long. The next thing
that happened was a telephone call from him to Dame
Beatrice. Apart from arresting Effie Winters, he had also
pulled in Chettle and Batcombe for the man-trap incident and
the call was a request to Dame Beatrice to go to the police
station, sit in on his interviews with them and put questions to
them herself if she saw the need.

'What if the lads turn dumb insolent,' said Innes, 'and refuse
to answer any questions at all? They would be within their
rights.'

'They will answer my godmother's questions,' said Mary.
We had to wait a couple of hours or more before we could find
out whether she was right. When Dame Beatrice returned it
was with what appeared to be a straightforward although a
somewhat bizarre story which the lads had told her.

For one thing, both were adamant that there had been no
theft from the museum. The man-trap, the buttons and the

smocks had all been lent to Hamid by the curator. They stuck
to this unlikely story and backed it up to some extent by
saying that when he knew of Hamid's injuries the curator had
covered himself by reporting that the man-trap had been
stolen, although, curiously enough, he had never suggested
that his employee, Chettle, was the thief.

Hallicks dealt with the situation by detailing a detective-
sergeant to go to the folk museum and question the curator.
He returned with only a partial refutation of Chettle's story.
The articles had been stolen, but Chettle had not been
suspected.

'How would he have got a thing as big and heavy as a
man-trap and two full-sized smocks out of the museum
without being detected?' the curator had asked. As for the doll,
that had been abstracted long before the other items disappeared. It had been on open show and was not in a case. They
assumed that some little girl had taken a fancy to it as they
had had various school parties to visit the museum. The doll,
although an unusual one, was not of intrinsic value and did
not form part of a collection of dolls, so they had turned a
blind eye to the theft and had not reported it until the other
things had been taken. Chettle had keys to the museum and
although there had been no signs of breaking and entering, the
thief must have had a car, which Chettle did not possess.

Having heard this story, Hallicks went into conference with
Dame Beatrice and pointed out that, on the strength of it, he
had no option but to believe the lads. There were still Dame
Beatrice's questions to put, however, and these concerned the
actual setting of the man-trap and their story that Hamid had
actually asked that this should be done. Then she asked what
they had been doing in Lower Gushbrook on the morning of
the Bounds procession.

They both (questioned separately) stuck to it that they had
had the curator's permission to borrow the man-trap and the
smocks for some theatricals which Hamid was staging at the
university. It was only when they had met him again that
they learned that the man-trap was to be set in his father's
woods. At first they repeated that they had had nothing to do
with this, but Dame Beatrice broke down their defence by

quoting from the notes she had taken at her first meeting with them at Innes's house.

'I was told,' she said, 'that the person who was caught in it was the person it was meant for and that everybody (which, I take it, means you and your friends) knew that. You have asserted that Hamid Aziz asked you, which I have no doubt means bribed you, to procure the man-trap and to let him know exactly where it was set. I shall get him to confirm that you set it.' She had then returned to the question of their activities at Lower Gushbrook, but here she drew blank.

They did not deny that they had been to that village on Bounds Sunday, but swore (and stuck to it) that they had merely been out for a spin on Batcombe's motorcycle.

'Ah, yes,' she said, 'the motorcycle which you bought with Hamid's money. It must have been a substantial payment.'

'We was taking a pretty big risk,' said Batcombe unwisely.

'In setting a man-trap in the sheikh's woods? Yes, I think you were,' said Dame Beatrice.

Out-manoeuvred, Batcombe, who had made a slip which she thought the cunning and more astute Chettle (psychopath or not) would have avoided, maintained for the next few minutes a stolid silence which he broke to say:

'You can't do nothing without Mr Hamid prosecutes, and we got witnesses, so he won't.'

'His father might,' Dame Beatrice pointed out. 'Did Hamid give you any reason for requiring the man-trap to be set?'

'No, he never.'

'So we left it at that,' said Dame Beatrice, 'and there it will remain until I have seen Hamid again.'

'Suppose he still won't talk to you?' said Mary.

'Then I shall give my questions to Superintendent Hallicks and tell him the answers I expect.'

'You mean you know the answers before you ask the questions?'

'Some of them. I repeat what I think I have said before. If not, I say it now. I can see only one reason for Hamid's deliberately stepping on to the man-trap. It must have been to enlist his father's sympathy. Hamid, I am certain, has committed some sin which is bound to come to light and he wants to bulwark himself against his father's wrath. What I must avoid if I can is having his father present at the interview, whether the Superintendent conducts it or whether I do.'

One thing of importance she had learned after Hallicks had let the two lads go came out a little later. This was a bit of circumstantial evidence on the strength of which, coupled with the noisy quarrel Effie Winters had had with her brother, Hallicks had arrested her.

The Winters had an ordinary household refrigerator but did not possess a deep freeze. However, it had not taken Hallicks long to find out that Effie had access to no fewer than three of these pieces of kitchen equipment. Because of his business associations with the sheikh, Winters had procured a part-time job for Effie as mending-maid to the young boy Murad. She was in request one whole day a week during term-time and two days a week during school holidays to look over his clothes, repair anything which required mending, make sure that anything which needed cleaning or laundering was despatched and, in short, to see that the child was kept bandbox-trim as befitted the boy who had so rich and proud a man as the sheikh for a father.

The sheikh's was a large household which needed a great deal of food. Effie was accustomed to go into the kitchen for mid-morning refreshments, her lunch and her tea, and must have known of the deep freeze which was not kept in the kitchen itself, but in an outhouse detached from the main building.

Hallicks, however, was thorough. Enquiries and tactful personal visits produced evidence that two other farmhouses, apart from Breedy's, possessed the equipment he was searching for, and Effie was on visiting terms with both. All the same, I thought Hallicks was taking a long shot in arresting Effie. Mary claimed optimistically that, as the wife of a magistrate, she felt that the law was not an ass and that, under it, no innocent person was likely to be convicted. She felt certain that Effie was innocent.

A different opinion came from Martha Lorne, who made the arrest an excuse for calling on us.

'*So* unlikely that a mistake has been made,' she said. 'The police have to be so careful about that kind of thing nowadays.'

'Superintendent Hallicks is still – what do they call it? – pursuing his enquiries, which he would not be doing if he could be sure that poor Effie was guilty,' said Mary.

'There *is* such a thing as looking for enough evidence to secure a conviction,' said Innes in an aside to me. Martha realised that he had spoken, although I doubt whether she had caught his words. From the window side of the room she said,

'I suppose Effie Winters will be remanded in custody when she comes before you and Lord Maumbury.'

'Not a doubt of it,' he said. 'We've already remanded her once.'

'It seems to me that the W.I. would be well employed raising money against her trial, if we want to help her,' said Martha. 'I suppose she is bound to come to trial?'

'There is time for fresh evidence to be unearthed,' said Mary. 'Hallicks is still busy, as I've already said.'

'There was the quarrel with her brother.'

'And, if she gets off, his insurance money,' said Innes.

'And, of course, she does have a rather suspect alibi,' said I, contributing my quota.

'Well, there you are!' said Martha in what sounded to me a triumphant tone. When she had gone, I hinted (very reluctantly, I admit) that it was more than time I went home. Mary received the suggestion not with the polite regret which, in a hostess, is often tantamount to saying, 'I should think so, too!' She looked genuinely concerned and even slightly alarmed. The latter she hastened to explain.

'Look, Mike darling, I want two men in the house until all this peculiar business is cleared up. Whoever heard, in these days, of people getting caught in man-traps and human bodies being put in deep freezes? It's horrible.'

'In the days when man-traps were in common use, there would hardly have been deep freezes,' said Innes, speaking lightly but looking at her rather anxiously, I thought. She stuck to what appeared to be her point.

'Dame Beatrice is a great responsibility while she stays here.

There will have been all sorts of gossip about her. There always is in this place when people have visitors who stay longer than overnight. Her reputation as a Home Office psychiatrist is bound to be known all over the village by now. What is the murderer going to think, once the information about what and who she is gets around to him? You *must* stay, Mike, and help cope.'

'So you really don't believe Effie is guilty?' I said.

'I'd be very glad, old man,' said Innes, 'if you would stay. Her next move, as I understand it, is to have another go at young Hamid. Between ourselves, Hallicks isn't all that excited about having arrested Effie Winters. It's the transportation of the body to Lower Gushbrook that bothers him. He told me privately that he was keeping a very open mind.'

'Those village lads were certain that the man-trap caught the person it was meant for,' said Mary.

'Yes, and that Hamid insisted upon being told exactly where it was and deliberately stepped on it. Strange, if true,' I said. 'He must have known it was a foolhardy thing to do.'

'You don't think it was his idea to attempt to establish an alibi for the time of the murder, do you?' asked Mary. 'Such a thought *might* have come to a desperate inexperienced boy if he had killed Winters either by design or accident.'

'Seems very far-fetched to me. Besides, why would *he* want to murder Winters?' asked Innes.

'Well, somebody tried to shoot Winters and we know now that Hamid was in the neighbourhood at the time that happened. He could have been the marksman. Effie might – just *might* – put a knife in her brother's back, but I'm certain she didn't fire that shot,' said Mary.

'That's why Hallicks is still pursuing his enquiries, I suppose,' I said.

CHAPTER 12

HAMID AZIZ COMES CLEAN

Whether it was because young Hamid had told Dame Beatrice that he would not answer questions put to him by a woman, or whether it was a reward to me for having given her the important clue which had resulted in the discovery of Winters's body in the punt, I did not ask. Dame Beatrice joined me while I was wandering round Innes's garden and made me her deputy. I was to memorise a list of questions she wanted to be put to the young Arab and write down the answers if Hamid's mood permitted me to record him on paper. If he jibbed, I was to do the best I could to remember what had been said.

'For, of course,' she observed, 'any one question and answer may lead to some disclosure which I have not foreseen, and then the conversation may take a different turn from that which we have planned. Are you good at extempore invention, Mr Michael?'

'I expect so,' I answered, with a confidence I did not feel. I thought of the times I had rehearsed in my mind an interview or an argument, only to find, when it came to the actual confrontation with my opposite number, that none of my carefully rehearsed speeches or arguments (particularly the arguments) had the least force or could be related in any way to the point at issue.

My first real facer came as soon as I was allowed into Hamid's private room, for there in the bed I thought I saw my young would-be suicide of the plank bridge. I was, of course, mistaken, particularly as he did not recognise me. A second's thought convinced me that it was the farmer's son, after all, whom I had encountered. To my surprise, Hamid seemed pleased to see me. I suppose he was well enough now to be suffering from boredom. I opened the conversation by saying that spring was a lovely season.

'In my walks in the woods I was luckier than you seem to have been,' I said. He smiled. In spite of a purplish tinge in his olive cheeks he was a handsome young specimen, if you like curling, sensuous lips, large, moist-looking brown eyes, a small silky moustache and long, rather greasy hair, although not much of his hair was visible because his head was still bandaged.

'Oh,' he said, 'the man-trap, yes. No doubt that was foolish of me. If so, I have paid for my folly. On the other side of the coin, however, I have had better luck.'

'Your father has forgiven you?' I asked, seizing upon a chance to put to him one of Dame Beatrice's questions, although it was not the first on the list I had memorised. He looked amused rather than startled, and a little colour came into his cheeks.

'Well! What do you know?' he said. It appeared to be a genuine question rather than the usual American-style exclamation, and I decided to treat it as such, hoping that I would not be upsetting Dame Beatrice's probably carefully arranged chessboard by so doing.

'What I know is mostly surmise,' I said. 'My only real piece of information (which I have been able to check, I must tell you) is that although you received your injuries on that Tuesday evening, you were in this neighbourhood some days earlier. That is to say, you left your train and, incidentally, your luggage, on the Sunday.'

'You know a great deal, I see. I will tell you the rest. Now that my father has forgiven me, I have nothing to fear, and neither has Peter Chettle.'

'What makes you mention Chettle?'

'Oh, that is where the man-trap came from. I heard that he had it. It was my idea that he should set it for me. I am sure that is not news to you. I do not think I covered my tracks very well. Tell me some news. I am so bored here.'

I told him of the story we had heard about Farmer Breedy and his son, and I remarked that when I entered the room I thought at first it was young Bob Breedy in the bed.

'The lad had his troubles,' I said, 'and a strict father much, I imagine, like yours.'

'And what were his troubles?' asked Hamid. 'You know, there is an English poet named Housman who wrote much about young men and their troubles. I would call him a universal poet, for all young men have the same troubles – wars and crimes and women and violent, relentless friend-ships, and sadnesses they cannot account for. It is all part of adolescence and it is very significant and painful while it lasts.'

I had outgrown the nostalgia of *A Shropshire Lad* and the *Last Poems* long enough ago, but I remembered my own youthful reaction to them and felt sympathy with Hamid, for his gazelle's eyes were fixed on mine as though in search of reassurance that the particular emotions which A. E. Housman had evoked would pass with the passing of time.

'You were going to tell me a story,' I reminded him. 'I have a particular reason for needing it, because, of course, the man-trap is a police matter and so is the murder.'

He surprised me by saying that he knew nothing about a murder, but he explained that, in a private room, he had had no contact with the other patients, that he had not felt equal to reading the papers and that the doctors and nurses had been keeping him so quiet that nothing of an exciting nature had reached him. His father had sent every day to enquire about his progress and he had had two visits from him. The first, by doctor's orders, had been very short, and at the second, which was very recent, he had confessed to his father that he was married to an English girl.

Dread of having his father find out about this *mésalliance* on account of racial and, more important, religious grounds, had caused Hamid to contemplate self-destruction, for somehow Winters (the boy almost spat as he mentioned the name) had got hold of the truth and had been blackmailing him during the whole of the summer vacation.

'But how could he have found out?' I asked. 'I suppose your wife is not a local girl?'

'I did what my religion forbids, but at college it is not always easy to live by the Koran.'

'You got drunk, and talked in your cups, I suppose,' I said. 'It's happened before. You should have told Winters to go to hell. Don't you realise, you silly young clot, that if Winters had

dared to go to your father with such a story all he would have
got was the hell of a beating-up from your father's guards? He
would never have risked that. He was simply taking you for a
ride.'

'But, after the beating-up, he could still have proved his
point.'

'It would never have come to that, I tell you. I suppose you
were ass enough to drink *here*, at the local pub.'

'It was standing the rounds that did it,' said Hamid, who
seemed to be accepting my avuncular strictures with surprising
meekness. 'At college we give parties, but we do not stand
rounds.'

'I know how pernicious this standing of rounds can be,' I
said, my mind going back to an occasion on which I had been
a member of a Rugby football club and had nearly passed out
for good and all. 'Why didn't you take up residence again at
college at the beginning of this term?'

'I was too much worried and afraid. I thought I would come
back and keep an eye on Winters.'

'But I thought term had begun a week or more before you
came back. We – and this includes the police – know quite a
bit about your movements, you see.'

'Yes, I see. I spent the days with my wife, but then, as I tell
you, I wanted to be where Winters was. I suppose I wanted to
keep him in my sights.'

'Somebody did so by putting a bullet through his hat. How
did you get to know him in the first place?' I asked, without
giving him time to ask the obvious question, which, in any
case, I could not answer.

'Oh, he was often at Bourne Farley. There was land my
father wanted to buy and Winters was the negotiator,'
explained Hamid.

'Farmer Breedy was the other party, I believe.' At this,
Hamid opened his eyes very wide indeed.

'You *do* know it all,' he said. 'Winters told me – but not my
father, who is too honourable a man to enquire into ways and
means if these are dubious. . . .'

This struck me as being such an original way of defining an
honourable man that I laughed and said, 'So Winters knew

how to put the screw on Breedy as well as on you, did he?'

'My information,' said Hamid, in a tone of dignified rebuke for what, apparently, he regarded as a flippant attitude on my part, 'does not go so far as that, but Winters seemed certain that he could persuade Breedy to sell Long Fallow to my father.'

'Be that as it may, what did you do with yourself between the Sunday you came back and the Tuesday when you stepped on the man-trap? I have reasons for asking.'

He said that I was beginning to alarm him and, although he said it mockingly and with a smile, I think he meant it. I wondered, not for the first time, whether the man-trap incident was not so much an appeal for his father's sympathy as an alibi for the murder of Winters. We had established that Winters could have been murdered as early as the Tuesday night and his body put into cold storage until a convenient time came to bury it, but, if Effie Winters, her quarrel with her brother and what Hallicks thought was her contrived alibi were discounted, there was no reason, so far as I could see, why Winters should not have been killed as soon as he left the sheikh's premises following the shot through his hat: that is to say, long before dark.

Granted this, then, if Hamid claimed to have come in by train at six o'clock on the Tuesday instead of on the previous Sunday, as we know is what actually happened, his alibi for the time of Winters's death could have been stronger. However, as I argued to myself, surely an intelligent young man such as, in spite of some youthful follies, I took Hamid to be, would have realised that a simple enquiry at the station would have established the day of his arrival, particularly since he had been so spectacularly loaded with luggage, luggage which he had left in the booking-clerk's charge. Against this, Hamid might have felt that nobody would think of making enquiries at the station as to the day of his arrival and, of course, on my first visit there, it had not occurred to me to do so.

'I'm afraid I'm tiring you,' I said, 'but we would like to have a clear account from you as to how you spent the time between the Sunday and the Tuesday.'

'Did that old woman send you?'

'Well, you refused to talk to her, so, as the matter is of great importance and she is attached to the Home Office, it was decided that I should deputise for her. You see, there is something which you do not appear to know. In fairness to yourself and the person who is now in custody, I think you should be put in the picture.'

'By our religion,' he said, smiling, 'we do not put human beings in pictures.'

I smiled in my turn and said that I did not believe all their artists had kept to the letter of the law. He became grave again and asked:

'Is Peter Chettle in custody?'

'No. It is Miss Winters.'

'I don't know her.'

'She is Winters's sister. She is suspected of murdering him.'

He looked incredulously at me.

'Winters is dead?'

'Dead and buried.'

'No wonder my father has forgiven me.'

It sounded an extraordinary remark. I suppose it made sense to him; it made none to me. However, it certainly started the ball rolling, for he began to talk in such a non-stop stream that my shorthand had all its work cut out to keep up with him.

He began with his courtship and subsequent marriage and I learned that the girl was not the tobacconist's assistant, the local barmaid or the landlady's daughter, those stock characters in undergraduates' personal dramas, but a history student at one of the women's colleges. They had slept together, boated and walked together, talked, gathered wild flowers, made love – all this, according to Hamid, in the most idyllic and delightful manner – but the girl insisted upon legalising the proceedings.

'And I was so much in love,' explained Hamid, 'that I put out of my mind my father and my religion and we are man and wife. Then, of course, as I told you, I got drunk here at the pub with Winters and some others and gave myself away. I have wrestled with my thoughts and my fears while I have been paying Winters the hush-money, and then I made up my mind for suicide, and then I thought my father might soften his heart because of the man-trap and then I would confess and ask his forgiveness and swear to make my wife a Mohammedan.'

When he had arrived at the station and had parked his baggage, he had strolled down the road to kill time until the station taxi returned. At this point I interrupted him.

'You mean you hung about because you had made an appointment to meet Chettle,' I said.

He laughed and gave me what I took to be an Arab gesture of respect.

'Now why do you say that?' he asked.

'Because, wherever you stayed that Sunday night and on the Monday and all day Tuesday, it was not in these parts, or somebody would have recognised you and commented to somebody else and so on. You had to make contact with Chettle and finalise the plans for setting the man-trap. I cannot compliment you on your choice of an ally.'

'There were two of them. Chettle came on Batcombe's motorcycle.'

'Oh, yes, of course.'

'We made our arrangements and then I got rid of them and waited for the taxi to come back to the station. I stayed at the hotel in Ropewalk and did not go out until dusk on the Tuesday evening. I came back by taxi – a cab from the station at Ropewalk, so that the driver would not know me – got out of the cab by my father's gates and walked into the woods and on to the man-trap, for Chettle and Batcombe had been as good as their word and set the trap almost at the spot agreed upon.'

'Almost?'

'I was dragging my feet and wondering whether, after all, I could go through all that agony when – bingo! – I was caught. I fainted with pain and shock and how I came by the clout on the head which made me continue to lose consciousness until I came to, here in the hospital, I don't know, and it does not matter now.'

'It matters if Chettle and Batcombe were in hiding near by and thought it might be as well to silence you for good and all,' I said grimly. He shook his head and grimaced as the emphatic movement hurt him.

'I paid them well,' he said simply. 'Mercenaries are always faithful.'

'Well, I can't quote from the Koran,' I said, 'but there is a book wherein I have read: "The hireling fleeth because he *is* an hireling." That doesn't say much for your mercenaries.'

' "These, in the day that Heaven was falling," ' he quoted back at me.

' "And took their wages and are dead," ' I reminded him, 'and so is Winters. One of these days, too, I would not be surprised if Batcombe's motorcycle does duty as Exhibit A in a trial for murder.'

'You think those two killed Winters?'

'Well, I don't believe his sister killed him. It was not, in my opinion, a woman's crime.'

'Not a crime at all,' he said. 'There is no crime in killing a rat. I might have done it myself if I were not afraid of the English law. But – life imprisonment? No, not unless my honour was involved.'

'You say that you were unconscious until you came to in this hospital bed,' I reminded him. 'How, then, did Wally Halstock find you and release you? I have been to the place where the man-trap was set. It is well away from the main path through the woods and that is the path Wally would have followed on his way to work. I suppose, although you were unconscious, you must have been groaning.'

Even as I said this, I felt considerable doubt. Even if a person who is totally unconscious is also able to groan, I thought of the distance the Superintendent, Dame Beatrice and I had penetrated into the woods to the place where Wally had freed Hamid from the man-trap, and I doubted whether any groans would have reached Wally's ears as he tramped the main path. Even if they had, I doubted whether a country lad with a damaged brain would have thought of investigating the sounds. Brought up and nourished on superstition, he would have been frightened enough to break into a run and get out of the woods as soon as he could, I thought.

I had put almost none of Dame Beatrice's questions directly, but I felt that Hamid had answered them without prompting. I also felt that I had gained items of information which her questions would not have elicited.

'Of course,' I said, when I had told her the tale and had read out the shorthand notes I had taken, 'as I see it, there is nothing against the theory that Hamid himself may be Winters's murderer. He says he did not get here that Tuesday until dusk, but there is nothing, so far, to substantiate that.'

'There is the Ropewalk taxi-driver,' she pointed out. 'No doubt Superintendent Hallicks will have no difficulty in finding him. Hamid is a striking-looking young man and a taxi-driver would remember him.'

'Certainly. But if it was proved that Hamid was lying about the time of day, it could be he who took the pot-shot which missed its mark and then he could have followed Winters up when Winters left Bourne Farley, stabbed him and still have carried out the man-trap business to provide himself with an alibi.'

'Hiding the body in whose deep-freeze?' asked Innes sardonically.

'His father's, of course,' said Mary, backing me up. 'Whatever Hamid had done, his father would have stood by him, I'm sure. Besides, with the sheikh's huge cars and the sheikh's bodyguard of huge men, transporting the body from wherever Hamid did the killing would have presented no difficulties at all.'

'Thank you, darling,' I said.

'Oh, yeah?' said Innes. 'And whose bright idea was it to bury Winters in that punt? The sheikh has acres of ground of his own where he can bury what he likes and no questions asked and nobody to split on him.'

'Chettle and Batcombe buried the body, of course,' said Mary.

'Well, they do seem to be well mixed up in the business,' I said.

'I can't imagine the sheikh putting the slightest confidence in either of them.' said Innes. 'Chettle, if not Batcombe, would rat at the slightest sign of trouble.'

'Not if he was paid enough and promised more for every

month he kept his mouth shut,' said Mary. I thought of Hamid's 'I pay them well,' and wondered. Does one balance a monthly income, however princely, against a possible life sentence? Bank robbery is one thing, unless it results in a killing. Accessory to murder, in my book, is quite another.

I looked at Dame Beatrice, but she did not join in the discussion.

CHAPTER 13

MARTHA LORNE

'He's protecting somebody,' said Hallicks, when he heard my story. 'Who would deliberately walk into a man-trap?'

Dame Beatrice pointed out that Hamid's action, according to what he himself had confessed to me at the interview, was not, in the end, either voluntary or deliberate. He had been caught by the horrible device because Chettle had set the thing a little nearer the main path than had been agreed upon and therefore Hamid, already in two minds about going through with his grisly project, had trodden on the man-trap unawares.

There remained the question of who had crept up and hit the helpless boy over the head and whether this had been a misguided act of intended mercy by keeping him unconscious and therefore putting him out of his agony for a time, or whether, as both Innes and Hallicks himself thought more likely, it was a deliberate attempt to kill him before he could grass on those who had caused his injuries. As Innes pointed out, they must have been paid their money, or Batcombe could not have afforded to buy a motorcycle. Presumably they thought they had nothing more to gain from Hamid and, because they had not set the trap in the agreed spot, but had forced him to walk into it whether he wanted to, in the end, or not, they must have believed that he would shop them to the police.

As for accounting for his presence in his father's woods at night, Innes went on, what could be easier than for Hamid to explain that he had an assignation with a girl? It would have been a cast-iron reason to give because everybody would have believed him.

Unfortunately for Hamid, my interview with him had produced a motive for the murder of Winters at his hands.

Blackmail is an ugly crime. Hamid's admitted fear of his father and his underlying other fear that there was always a chance that Winters, in his cups or otherwise, might let out the fact of the mixed marriage, this coupled with what must have been a smouldering, deep-down hatred of the man who had him in his power, provided a much sounder motive for murder than the one so far attributed to Effie Winters.

'I must have a go at him,' Hallicks said. 'These Arabs hold life cheaper than we do. If he's been under pressure from Winters, he probably decided to release himself by getting rid of the fellow. It would not have seemed to him a wrong thing to do, perhaps, and off the record I don't know that I blame him, but of course in my job I can't allow that to make any difference. I'll give him a day or two to forget his talk with you, sir. Meanwhile I shall pull in those two lads and knock a confession out of them. It shouldn't be difficult. Master Batcombe will soon come clean, even if that young snake Chettle tries to wriggle off the hook.'

Under a relentless, although (from what I knew of Hallicks) a perfectly fair, inquisition both boys, interviewed separately, admitted to setting the man-trap, but remained immovable in their argument that Hamid had paid them for doing so and had promised them immunity from the law if they did as he wished.

Their answers to Hallicks's further questions failed to tally on only one point. Batcombe alleged – and stuck to the assertion – that, apart from the fact that it was to be set in the sheikh's woods, he had never been told of the exact spot which had been chosen. He added that he had never believed that Hamid would go through with the project – 'anybody would chicken out of a fool stunt like that, when it comes to the crunch, sir' – but he thought perhaps the contraption might catch a rabbit or even a deer, certainly not a man who had walked into it deliberately.

Chettle was obliged to admit to an agreement with Hamid as to where the man-trap was to be placed, but asserted vehemently that he had kept strictly to the agreement and that, if Hamid had walked himself into the trap, it was of his own choice and of his own free will.

Hallicks did not believe him, but he could not shake him. He dismissed Batcombe with a solemn warning that he might be wanted again for police questioning and said that it would be better for him if he did not attempt in the meantime to leave the neighbourhood. Then he turned his big guns on Chettle.

The youth held out, however, giving cheeky answers learned from television programmes featuring teenage hooligans in conflict with 'the pigs', and refused to be worn down and penned by what, said Innes, who told us the story he had received from Hallicks, 'he no doubt regarded as "pig's" logic. At any rate, Chettle refused to admit hitting Hamid over the head.

'Went back to see if there was anything I could do,' he said. 'Didn't know whether he was catched in the trap or not, did I? When I got there he was a-groaning sommat cruel and I done my best let him out. It were plaguey dark in them woods, though, and I didn't have nothing but my little torch to see by, and even then I has to lay it down on the ground so as to have both hands free to pull the trap open. Well, I can't shift them iron jaws, can I? They was too deep into his leg. So I goes and knocks up my mate, but he don't want no part in it.'

Hallicks suggested that Batcombe had not been asked to render any more assistance and came back to the point at issue, which was that Chettle had deliberately hit Hamid over the head with the intention of killing him. This the youth again strenuously denied and asserted that it was not Batcombe to whom he referred, but Wally Halstock.

'His dad answered the door,' he said, 'so I tells him the tale, don't I? – and all he says is as it serves that Arab scum right, as it were his evidence at the inquest on Mr Lorne as put Breedy's lorry in the clear and cut the compensation money down to nowt. Wally come to the door when he heared his dad and me talking, and us fixed up as Wally would give a look at the trap on his way to work in the morning, which he done.'

'Strange that he could set Hamid Aziz free if you couldn't,' said Hallicks; but to this Chettle replied that Wally was very much the stronger of the two of them, a statement which Hallicks could not gainsay.

One thing which had resulted from all the excitement, combined with the visit of Dame Beatrice and myself to Strode Hillary, had been the curtailing of Mary's and Innes's social life. They were a gregarious couple and had a good many friends, both in Strode Hillary and outside it. Except for the visits of Martha Lorne, who had become somewhat of an incubus and was not, except in her own estimation, a close friend, and the dinner with the Maumburys, the social activities of my brother and his wife had been non-existent.

When, therefore, they received an invitation to the birthday party of a child whose parents lived on the other side of the county, both Dame Beatrice and I urged that they accept it. Dame Beatrice said that she would like to go home for the day and telephoned her chauffeur to this effect, and I admitted to a hope that I might get a book out of my visit and therefore would be glad of an opportunity to explore more of the countryside in search of background material.

'And for that,' I said, 'I need to be on my own.'

We saw Dame Beatrice off, then I drove my own car to the garage, filled up the tank and decided to let my fancy lead me. I felt that I knew the countryside to the south-east of the village sufficiently well for my purpose, so I headed west and a little to the south and bypassed the turning which led to the viewpoint from which Innes had given me my first real aspect of the local countryside.

Leaving this turning on my right, I followed a good road which had a surface slightly in need of repairs, until I came to a village almost large enough to be called a town, and here I found I had a choice of routes.

So far as I was concerned, the choice was arbitrary, so I took a righthand fork and soon found myself in what I can describe, without any fear of contradiction, as a typical Dorset lane.

It was wet from rain which we had not had in Strode Hillary, and wound this way and that as the contours of the hills suggested. It was so narrow that I wondered what would happen if I encountered a farm vehicle or another car (for there were no passing-places), and either the lane was enclosed by high banks topped by shorn hedges or else it serpentined through an open countryside of hills, valleys and pasture of an unbelievable, almost startling green.

The banks and the roadside were covered in wild daffodils (now, like those in Mary's tubs, past their best, but still a bright show of sunlight colour) and the even brighter butter colour of the lesser celandine.

Then, on all the banks there were primroses, and where I reached a little church at which I pulled up, there was a tiny brook, shining and freely flowing, growing cresses and burbling over stones.

I went into the church and also walked all round it. When I got back to the car I looked at my watch and decided that by the time I reached Strode Hillary, where I intended to make some notes for my novel, it would be lunch-time. There was no village near the church, which was situated on a knoll completely covered in daffodils, primroses and the ubiquitous lesser celandine, all growing amid that incredible verdure. I was loth to leave the spot, but drove off at last. I was approaching the hill-tunnel near the viewpoint of Strode Hillary when I was aware of a woman who, almost at the entrance to the tunnel, was thumbing a lift. On the whole – in fact, with very few exceptions – I do not stop to pick up persons thumbing lifts. For one thing I do not see why I should purchase, insure and maintain a car in order to give casual strangers a free ride, and to go on with, there are the safety risks, both to the passenger and myself. Young girls frighten me and so, of course, do youths with flick knives and revolvers. At least, the *thought* of them frightens me enough to refuse them a lift. However, a middle-aged woman is a different matter. Besides, I recognised the woman. It was Martha Lorne. I pulled up well short of the entrance to the tunnel and tooted the horn. She came towards me and I stretched out and opened the car door.

'Ah,' she said, getting in beside me, slamming the car door with unnecessary force and pulling the seat-belt across her bosom, 'this is very nice of you, Michael. Can you go to Cross Street?'

'If you will direct me,' I said. 'Is it a turning out of the Square?'

'Well, no. It's in Ropewalk. I have a very important appointment there. I tried to get a taxi but there is only the one and he was booked up, so I called at Mary's to ask whether you or Innes could take me, but there was nobody at home.'

'Wouldn't you have stood more chance of a lift if you had walked back into the town?' I asked.

'Well, yes, but I didn't really want any of the W. I. members to know my business, and one of them would have been sure to spot me and wonder why I was trying to get a lift. Everybody minds everybody else's business in a small place like this. One can't keep anything to oneself.'

'No, I suppose not,' I said. I was not at all pleased at the idea of spending time to take her to Ropewalk. I wanted to get my notes down while my impressions were fresh in my mind and I badly wanted my lunch, which I had planned to have at the Stag. Besides, I had a foreboding that she would want me to wait in Ropewalk while she transacted her business and then would expect me to drive her home.

Fortunately this did not occur. She directed me when we reached the outskirts of Ropewalk, and when we arrived at what she claimed was her destination, I was surprised to see Farmer Breedy standing on the pavement at the rear of a vintage Rolls Royce.

I got out, went round to Mrs Lorne's side and opened the car door for her. She stepped on to the pavement and I realised for the first time that she was unusually smartly dressed and was wearing a hat covered with velvet violets. Moreover, she was carrying a white handbag and a pair of violet-coloured gloves to match the hat.

Breedy made no attempt to come towards us. She joined him, climbed into the Rolls Royce and off they went. Making nothing of this (except that I felt a certain amount of surprise to be a witness to a meeting between such unlikely friends), I turned my car, thankful that there was no waiting about in Ropewalk to be done, and drove back to Strode Hillary.

Here I had lunch at the Stag, as I had planned, and then went to Innes's house to jot down my notes. It was still short of three o'clock, so I debated whether to use the afternoon for

further exploration or whether to draft a first chapter, always
a pleasant exercise because it begins a new enterprise and has
none of the complications which invariably crop up later, no
matter how carefully one thinks one has plotted the book.

In the end, after making myself coffee – that which the Stag
supplied had proved to be undrinkable – I decided that a fine
Spring afternoon would be wasted indoors, and that while I
was on my own without the distraction of Mary's society (for I
had no illusions about the extent to which she both attracted
and distracted me) I ought to collect as much background
material as I could while I had such a splendid opportunity.

I went up to Innes's library where he had an up-to-date
collection of Ordnance maps, and decided, after a quarter of
an hour's browsing, upon two villages to the south, both of
which were on the coast.

There could not have been a greater contrast between two
places so few miles apart. I went first to Sandbay. It had once
been the port for Ropewalk, and still possessed a tidy little
harbour, but this was chiefly taken up now by small yachts
and cabin cruisers and there was talk, I had heard, of building
a marina there.

For the rest, the place looked both brash and unfinished.
Holiday flats; some more permanent residences; a hotel with a
broad terrace looking over the open sea; a concreted broad-
walk along the sea front; and an outbreak of ice-cream kiosks,
stalls selling postcards and toys, a hot-dog stand, and a booth
which sold newspapers and periodicals, combined to take
attention away from any attractions which the coastal scenery
might have to offer.

However, at that time of year there was ample parking
space along the front. I locked the car and left it, took a brisk
walk – for the air was extremely fresh – and on my return I
took another look at the harbour before I drove off for the
village of Compton Bewley.

Here I found a place to leave the car, and then I walked the
narrow streets and delighted in their unexpected charm. There
were thatched cottages with gardens full of daffodils, stone-
built houses with mullioned windows, Georgian residences of
austere façade and beautifully proportioned doorways. Every-

where (with the children all in school) there was a tranquil air as though the place had gone to sleep at the turn of the century and had let the troublous years of wars and industrial disputes, the era of the aeroplane and of space travel, motorways and the Common Market go by without the village knowing or caring anything about these changes.

I finished my walkabout at a road bridge which crossed a pleasant little stream. It ran past the school and the church and on the opposite side of the road it skirted the gardens of some of the houses. I leaned on a wooden rail and could see weeping willows and a beautiful, flowering magnolia tree. As I stood there someone joined me. Knowing that I had no acquaintances in the place, I took no notice until he spoke. It was Hallicks.

'Good afternoon, Mr Lockerbie. Pretty little place, isn't it? I always reckon that this ranks with Cerne Abbas and Corfe Castle as one of the nicest little spots in the county. I used to live here as a boy, so when I can squeeze a free couple of hours, I come back.'

'Any more luck with Chettle and Batcombe?' I asked.

'Pulled them in, sir. They'll have to come up before the Bench. Can't overlook the fact that, apart from the actual man-trap, one of them, and I put my money on Chettle, tried to finish off the Arab boy. A real nasty little bit of work is our Master Chettle.'

'Nothing further come to light in the case of Winters, I suppose?'

'Nothing I can act on, no, sir. My mind runs on Breedy, though why it should I don't know, except that there's pub talk as Winters had the drop on Breedy's son Bob, but you'll have heard about that.'

'Talking of Breedy,' I said, 'I didn't know that he and Mrs Lorne were close friends.'

'Close friends? Where did you get that one from, sir?'

I described how Martha had thumbed me for a lift that midday and of my surprise when she met Breedy in a side street in Ropewalk and got into a car with him.

'Well, well!' he said. 'I wouldn't mind knowing what that was in aid of. I always thought – everybody thought – she blamed Breedy and his lorry for her husband's death. Well, that which you've told me is certainly a turn up for the book so far as I'm concerned. Glad you mentioned it, not that it solves any problems. Ah, well, I must be off. Here on your own, sir, I take it.'

'Yes. The other two were invited out and Dame Beatrice has gone home for the day to attend to correspondence or some such. I daresay she'll stay the night, but we're expecting her back quite shortly.'

He walked with me to where I had left my car. His own was close by. We passed a double-fronted house with mullioned windows and subsidiary stone transoms. It was a dignified and beautiful house dating, I thought, from the fifteenth or early sixteenth century. Hallicks, however, saw it with other eyes. It had a very narrow front garden, unfenced and abutting on to the street, and this patch of ground, which ran the whole length of the frontage, was a dense conglomeration of brilliant yellow, a mass of celandines. I liked the effect against the grey stonework, but it did not please Hallicks at all.

'Pity to see a nice old place neglected like that,' he said. 'In my time the Beckwiths had it. You wouldn't have seen weeds like that in *their* time.'

We got into our respective cars and I gave him the road, since presumably he had less time to spare than I had. I was in no hurry to get back to an empty house. I drove out to Lyme Regis, had my tea there and then cruised around by way of Axminster and Crewkerne and so back to Strode Hillary, where I dined at the Stag.

By the time I got indoors Mary and Innes were home again. Innes was cutting sandwiches, for they had not stayed for the birthday dinner at their friends' house.

'The party was really for the child and she wasn't going to be allowed to stay up for dinner,' said Mary, 'so we made that an excuse to come away. There was a children's party with twenty-four young guests and all their fathers coming to collect them at the end and have drinks with Ian, so we were quite glad to slip away. Children are very sweet, I suppose, but—'

'But definitely fatiguing,' said Innes. 'Are you cutting in on these sandwiches, Mike?'

'No. I've dined, thanks.'

'Then I think I've made enough. What I really need is a drink.'

'Well, any news?' asked Mary, when we had settled down. I described my day. My encounter with Martha Lorne was greeted with disbelief. Mary accused me of making the whole thing up. By this she referred to my transporting of Martha Lorne to Ropewalk and especially of her fraternisation with Farmer Breedy. Innes closed one eye and blew his cheeks out. Then he asked whether I could not think of a better leg-pull and stated that I was losing my grip.

'All right,' I said. 'Have it your own way. I may have been dreaming. The weather was fine. The Dorset hills and the brilliant green of the pasture and the hawthorn hedges, the beauty of the primroses, the wild daffodils, and the lesser celandines, the sound of the brook babbling over its stones and nourishing its wild cresses, and the lambs with their dams, and all that, may have addled my mind and hallucination may have set in, so have it your own way.'

'I believe he's serious,' said Mary, 'but why would Martha need to thumb a lift? She's on the phone and she's not so poor that she can't afford a taxi into Ropewalk.'

'It was booked up,' I said, 'as she explained. She indicated that her errand was urgent.'

'But she detests Breedy. She's often said so.'

'I thought she had never mentioned her husband's death to you.'

'She hadn't, but she did sometimes mention Breedy. We assumed he'd done her down over some deal or other,' said Innes.

'Well, if you ask me,' I said, 'the whole thing was reminiscent of a blushing and marvellously togged-up lady off with her cavalier to the registrar's office and the wedding breakfast.'

CHAPTER 14

A SHEIKH AND A SCHOOL

It turned out that Hallicks had arrested Chettle on another charge as well as for being concerned in the man-trap affair and for the strong suspicion that he had tried to kill Hamid. This was that he was the third man guilty of the local robberies. It was the caretaker at Fell Hall, who was still remanded awaiting (at his own request) trial before a Crown Court, who reported this. Apparently he was still trying to cover himself. He contended that his crime was a venial one, since all the valuables he had helped to steal had been recovered.

'But if he thinks a judge is likely to take a more lenient view than the local Bench would do, he's got another think coming,' said Hallicks. 'He was the receiver, as well as one of the burglars. In any case, the beaks would have sent him for trial if he had come up in front of them. They would have had no option. Still, he's doing the best he can for himself by shopping his mates right and left. We knew there must have been a third man involved.'

'I remember it was mentioned,' said Mary, when Innes recounted his conversation with Hallicks on the matter, 'but how could the police be sure?'

'Simple,' I said. 'I spotted two men in that car which passed me when I was coming away from Fell Hall. The third chap was the one in your kitchen when I got home. If that third man had been Chettle, I would have recognised him when Dame Beatrice interviewed those lads. I didn't recognise him, therefore he was not Chettle, so if Chettle was one of the burglars he was one of the chaps I saw in the car.'

'Simple indeed, when you know,' she said. 'Only one thing sticks in my mind, though. If the third man was Winters, as the caretaker claims, your aescription of the man in our kitchen doesn't tally.' She went on, 'Dame B. must have got up early this morning. I wanted to give her a second breakfast when she arrived from the Stone House at nine, but she wouldn't have any.'

'Oh, where is she, then?' I asked.

'At Bourne Farley, presumably. The sheikh's invitation came about twenty minutes before you came downstairs, you lazy man, and she went straight off in the biggest and most luxurious car that even the sheikh, I suppose, can supply. It appears that the hospital allowed Hamid to go home yesterday while we were all out, and I suppose Abdul wants a confrontation between my godmother and his son.'

'With himself as both touch-judge and referee,' said Innes.

'Anyway, she is invited to lunch there. Sheep's eyes, chunks of mutton, cushions on the floor, tear off the meat you fancy and eat with your fingers, I suppose.'

'Don't be disgusting,' said Mary. 'The sheikh sits up to table like every other civilised person.'

'Henry the Eighth sat up to table, but I wouldn't call his eating habits all that civilised,' retorted Innes.

'You've been seeing too many films, darling. What do you want to do today, Mike?'

'Go and ask questions at Lower Gushbrook Primary School,' I answered. 'I still regard that submerged punt as my prize item in the saga of dirty deeds in Dorset and I yearn to find out who did the initial gardening on it.'

'I thought we agreed that it was done when the murderer and his accomplice – whoever that turns out to be – buried Winters,' said Innes.

'I've been thinking about that, and about all that muck that was piled on top of the punt afterwards. We thought at first that whoever did that was trying to draw attention to the punt. We thought it was done by somebody who knew the body was there, but who wasn't prepared to go to the police and tell them so. That idea seemed all right at the time, but before Dame Beatrice and I got there that day with our trowels, she had already decided that the punt was a grave. The coal-dust and rubbish only confirmed her in that view.'

'She was suspicious when she saw Chettle and his pal fooling about there on the morning of Bounds Sunday,' said Mary. 'She suspected Chettle almost from the beginning of being concerned in the man-trap business. But what has made you doubtful about the plants in the punt, Mike? You've always been so pleased with yourself for spotting that they'd been changed.'

'I'm still pleased about it,' I said stoutly. 'I consider that I showed powers of observation and of memory far beyond the ordinary.'

Mary said, 'You clever boy! Take a bouquet!' She took the spring flowers from a vase and thrust them, dripping, into the open neck of my shirt. I grabbed her and held her and kissed her on the mouth. Innes took this better than I would have expected. All he said was:

'Unhand that woman and tell us why you've changed your mind about the punt. Why do you think now that the schoolchildren did the gardening?'

'It was always a possibility. It got mentioned, if you remember.'

'So?'

'Later we heard that Winters's body had been put into somebody's deep freeze. They wouldn't have done that if the burial had been carried out *before* I noticed that the plants had been changed. For some reason which, at present, we don't know, the murderer couldn't bury the body in the punt straight away, and my guess is that that was because the punt was under observation or else that somebody else was fooling about with it or had commandeered it for some reason.'

'The schoolchildren, you think?'

'I think it might be worth finding out,' I said. Mary had gone into the kitchen. She came back at this point and said,

'If you're going over to Lower Gushbrook, Mike, we'd better have lunch early. Those young children are probably dismissed at half-past three or a quarter to four, so you haven't got an awful lot of time.'

It is all very well to make up one's mind to invade other

people's premises in the interests of a little amateur detective work, but I had realised that I should need some reasonable excuse for troubling whoever was in charge of the school, so I had given thought to this. I decided to tell some part of the truth but not, of course, to mention anything connected with the murder unless whoever I spoke to at the school mentioned it first.

I had on me the membership card of one of the literary societies to which I belong, so, when I pulled up at the school entrance, I wrote on the back of the card under my signature: *Author doing local survey.*

It seemed that I had arrived at the end of the mid-afternoon playtime break, for lines of young children, officered by a man and two women teachers, were walking into the building. I waited at the gate and, as the last file was disappearing, the man approached me and asked whether he could help me.

'I am hoping to talk with the headmaster,' I replied.

'Are you a parent?'

'No.' I produced my card. He studied it.

'I thought you weren't a parent. I believe I know them all,' he said pleasantly. 'It's a headmistress, actually. Come this way. I'll find her for you.'

We went in by way of a little porch rather like the entrance to a village church. This led into a vestibule which appeared to be the children's washroom, for there were half a dozen washbasins, a receptacle from which paper towels could be pulled, and a large wire bin already more than half full of discarded towels. The teacher excused himself and left me, returning in a short time with a rather attractive-looking, brown-haired woman wearing a flowered overall. He went off, murmuring something about a craft lesson and left me with the girl.

'Good afternoon,' she said. 'Mrs Comyns is with a publisher's representative, so she wondered whether I could help as I'm free this period. You'd like this back, I expect.' She returned my membership card. 'I've sent for a couple of chairs. We don't run to a staff-room, I'm afraid. It's just as well. Our free periods are few and far between!'

Two small boys came through the doorway which obviously

led into a classroom, each carrying a chair. These they put down and we seated ourselves, but scarcely had we done so when a stream of five small children, each carrying a glass pot of the kind which usually holds fishpaste, came trooping up to the washbasins to empty out coloured water, rinse the pots and refill them from the taps.

'Oh, dear!' said the girl beside me. 'I'm afraid it will be like this for the next half-hour. Miss Prickett has got art.' (It sounded like a disease and possibly, with a class of young children, that is what it was!)

'I suppose we couldn't go and sit in my car?' I suggested. She gave me an appraising look and then she went over to one of the children and told her to tell Miss Prickett that Miss Seldon had had to go out for a few minutes and would Miss Prickett let Mrs Comyns know as soon as the gentleman in Mrs Comyns' room had gone.

These apparently important preliminaries completed, we went out to my car.

'You see, we're not supposed to leave the building during lesson times,' she said, 'unless we're taking P.E. or going out to Games.'

I unlocked, handed her in and we opened the windows.

'Well, now,' I said, taking out my notebook, 'I am preparing to make a local survey as a background to my next novel. I have been in the village more than once, and should like to use it as a setting.'

'Yes, it is pretty. I saw that your name is Lockerbie. Is that the name you write under?'

'Certainly.'

'I must see whether the County Library has got any of your books. I've never met an author before.'

As it was obvious that she had never heard of me before, either, I passed this over and settled down to business, for I realised that time was short. We exchanged some remarks and opinions about the village and the landscape and then I mentioned the punt.

'Goodness knows how long *that's* been there,' she said, 'or who put it there. I believe, in the days of Mr Sims (he was headmaster here until he retired some years ago) the children used to put up a flagpole in the punt and fly a Union Jack on special days – St. George's Day and the Queen's official birthday and so on – but Mrs Comyns thinks that is a waste of school time, so now we have a Mayday thing and do folk dances in the playground.'

'Is that the only function the punt was ever used for?' I asked. 'I am by way of being a bit of a botanist and on one of my visits here a short time ago I could not help noticing that the rather straggly, self-sown wild plants had been added to and a lot of tidying-up done.'

'That was before some vandals came along one evening and threw a lot of rubbish about. The children were heartbroken. Mr. Bell had been doing a Nature Project, you see, and they were to change the plants according to what they could find growing month by month, but, apart from the mess these wretched louts made, nobody likes the punt since there was that dreadful business of the police finding a dead body in it.'

From this point it was easy enough to go on. I mentioned that my brother was a magistrate and I got the all-important dates down in my notebook. At parting – she fled when she heard the bell which announced the end of the school day – I promised her a copy of my book when it came out, and I wrote down that promise so that it should not slip my mind.

I had seen a man whom I took to be the publisher's traveller. He had left the school premises about five minutes before the bell rang, so I was not surprised when, after the children had streamed out, a middle-aged lady in a dark dress and wearing glasses came up to the car. I got out and she greeted me with what seemed, in so calm and dignified a person, unusual deference. Authors, it seemed, took a high place in her conception of an oligarchy, for she mentioned the matter at once.

'I am so sorry I was engaged when you arrived, but I was busy ordering text-books. I should have asked you to advise me, shouldn't I? You must know all about that kind of thing.'

I disclaimed the possession of such knowledge, so, after hoping that Miss Seldon had been of assistance to me, she popped the inevitable question.

'I *wonder* whether I could persuade you to come and talk to the children one Friday afternoon? It would mean so much to them to see and hear a real author.'

'I expect to be recalled to London any day now,' I said. 'I have to see my publisher. He will want to know all about the Lower Gushbrook idea.' (A black lie, if ever I told one!)

'Oh, well, you'll be down here again soon, I'm sure,' she said brightly. 'I will keep a few dates open in my diary. I am sure we shall all look forward to hearing you. It does not *have* to be a Friday, of course, if that would not suit you.'

I made some modest, polite, non-committal noises which she appeared to think indicated willingness to place myself at her service, and she beamed, wished me luck with the book and went back into the building. Thankfully I reversed the car and made for Strode Hillary and a cup of tea.

Mary had arranged a dinner which could be left to look after itself – a casserole dish of some sort – as we did not know at what time to expect Dame Beatrice. She came back at soon after seven, however, and gave us a lively account of her day at Bourne Farley, although nothing, she thought, had resulted from it except that the sheikh had agreed to meet Hamid's wife on condition that she was prepared to become a Mohammedan.

'Father and son are reconciled,' said Dame Beatrice, 'and Hamid is to resume his studies as soon as he is well enough. I met his mother, who appears to be entirely Europeanised and would pass for a Frenchwoman.'

'What is the sheikh going to think when Hallicks unmasks the big guns and grills Hamid about the death of Winters?' asked Innes.

'My bet is that he'll put that off until Effie Winters is either brought to trial or released,' I said, 'and, in any case, I think that what I learned today may remove any suspicions that Hamid may have killed Winters.' I had already put Innes and Mary in the picture, although Innes had pointed out that the evidence I had collected from Miss Seldon only served to show that Hamid could not have buried Winters' body. It did not prove that he had not killed him.

After dinner Dame Beatrice and I went into conclave in the
library, leaving the other two downstairs to watch television,
and I gave her a full account of my visit to Lower Gushbrook
school.

'I wonder where all the coal-dust and ashes came from
which were heaped on the punt?' she said, when I had finished.
'Yes, and the rubble from the roadway. There is no way that I
can see for so much of that kind of thing to have been
transported by motorcycle, which is Chettle's means of getting
about.'

'You don't think, then, that Chettle and Batcombe were
bribed to bury the body if Hamid was the murderer?' (I
thought it would be interesting to act as Devil's Advocate to
see what she would say.)

'Let us check our dates again, so far as we know them.
Winters was certainly alive on the Tuesday before I came here
on the Friday. Tuesday was the morning somebody fired a
bullet through his hat.'

'Have you made up your mind who the rather ineffectual
marksman was?' I asked.

'Oh, there is no doubt who he was, Mr Michael. I am
certain he was young Breedy, Farmer Breedy's son. However, I
would not have called him ineffectual. The shot, I am
convinced, did what it was intended to do. It was a warning of
what Winters had to expect if he continued to persecute the
young man by attempting to blackmail him. I have no doubt
whatever that Winters guessed, even if he did not know, who
fired that shot. Had it really been intended to kill, it would
have done so. A farmer's son accustomed to shoot rabbits and
birds does not miss a target the size of a man. While I was at
Bourne Farley today I asked the sheikh about the incident. He
took me to the spot where he and Winters had been standing
when the shot was fired and then led me into the home
woodlands to what he thinks was the marksman's lair. Nobody
who was accustomed to shooting could have missed Winters
at such a distance if he had shot to wound or kill. Winters
and the sheikh were even standing still when the shot was
fired.'

'There could have been trees in the way.'

'The marksman may have been sheltering behind a tree, but, from what I saw, he could have got a shot in easily enough and made his escape while Winters was still examining the hole made in his hat.'

'If young Breedy was the marksman, how would he have known that Winters would be in the open at that particular time and so make a target of himself?'

'Because he knew all about the sheikh's negotiations to buy the piece of land called Long Fallow from his father. I think he followed all Winters's movements pretty closely and had no doubt that when Winters went to Bourne Farley it was to confer with the sheikh about that stretch of Breedy property. They must have had more than one meeting and it was this particular one which gave the harassed young man a chance to issue his warning.'

'Well, if you'll forgive me for saying so, Dame Beatrice, it's really all theory, isn't it?'

'Oh, yes,' she admitted, with the cackle which always disconcerted me, 'it is all theory, Mr Michael, so now to our dates, or shall I say our *moutons?*'

I took out my notebook and read aloud.

'Tuesday, the shot through Winters's hat. Winters almost certainly the thief I found in the kitchen at approximately half-past two. If he was the man I saw, Winters was certainly alive at that time. On the same day, or, rather, evening, Hamid stepped on to the man-trap, so, unless he had killed Winters before he did that, Hamid is in the clear.' I looked up. 'All right so far?'

'Admirable,' she said. 'Do please go on.'

'The trouble is,' I said, before I returned to my notes, 'that we can't prove whether Winters was alive or dead when Hamid stepped on to the trap. I still can't help thinking, you know, that he may have killed Winters a little earlier and that the man-trap was intended to give him an alibi.'

'Winters' body was deep-frozen until it could be buried. How could Hamid or his accomplices have managed that? Hamid himself could not have risked using the contraption at Bourne Farley, and it is difficult to imagine how Chettle and Batcombe could have had access to it. The sheikh's servants are many and, as foreigners in this country, are probably wary and suspicious.'

'You don't think Hamid could have been in cahoots with Effie Winters? She may not have committed the murder, but she seems to have been at loggerheads with her brother and we know that *she* could have had access to the deep freeze at Bourne Farley.' (I was still trying to probe Dame Beatrice's mind. She leered at me.)

'That, in itself, seems to me a very long shot, as my secretary would say. The body had to be taken to the deep freeze before it could be put into it,' she said, pretending to take me seriously. 'How could that have been managed, do you suppose?'

'The deep freeze is in an outhouse,' I said.

'I concede that. Who would have helped her, though? Clearly Hamid himself could not have done so. He was engaged in establishing his alibi.'

'Chettle or Batcombe or both?'

'In collusion with Effie Winters? They may have trusted Hamid and his undoubted ability to pay them, but a woman – and an indigent one at that? Youths of that age and background have a rooted intolerance towards women of mature years. They would not have trusted Effie as a fellow-conspirator, let alone as the moving spirit in a very dangerous enterprise.'

'Theory again,' I said, challenging her.

'Based on sound psychological principles and many years of interested observation, Mr Michael. I am inclined, wisely or not, to dismiss Chettle and Batcombe from the case. I have no doubt about their share in the man-trap incident, neither have I any doubt that it was Batcombe who insisted that Walter Halstock should be sent on Wednesday morning into the sheikh's woods to raise the alarm when he found Hamid caught in the man-trap. I am also sure that it was Chettle who returned alone on the Tuesday night and made the attempt to kill Hamid to secure, as he thought, his silence. There is one other thing, not that it is of the least importance now, except as a matter of interest. I have been told of your discovery of a hooded man in Mr Innes's kitchen. Will you describe him to me?'

I did my best, so far as I recollected my very brief acquaintance with the man.

'Young, sturdily built?' she said. 'It hardly tallies with what I have been told about Winters, does it?'

Mary had made the same point, I remembered. Had the caretaker only incriminated Winters because he knew the man was dead and could not defend himself? If so, of whom was Burrows so much afraid that he dared not give the name to the police? Did he suspect that this man was Winters' murderer?

CHAPTER 15

THE MONSTROUS REGIMENT
OF WOMEN

'Of course,' she went on, after I had told her that Miss
Seldon's story about the Nature project had confirmed at least
one of our theories, 'there are two lines of enquiry which
Superintendent Hallicks is pursuing. He is still looking for the
murder weapon and although he knows *how*, he does not know
where Winters was killed. It seems certain, I imagine, that
whether Effie Winters did the killing or not, it was not done in
Winters's own home. Murder by stabbing is not a pretty affair.
The traces of it would be almost impossible to disguise if the
stabbing took place within doors.'

'How about the garden?'

'With neighbours living so close that they had heard the
brother and sister quarrelling?'

So we went back to the dates in my notebook. Nothing
which happened before about three p.m. on that Tuesday
needed to enter into our calculations so far as the murder was
concerned. That day, however, had seen my first visit to Lower
Gushbrook. This had taken place before Mr Bell had begun
his Nature project on the punt. On my next visit, which had
been on the Friday of the same week, the project had been
begun and the gardening on the punt had been the work of
Bell and his young pupils, so the body had not been buried by
that time, but must have been either alive or in cold storage.
Effie Winters was either on a genuine visit or preparing her
alibi, but had not thought fit to report her brother's disappearance until the following Monday.

Winters had certainly been buried (and as stiff as a frozen
carcass of mutton, according to reports) before Dame Beatrice
and I saw all the débris which had been thrown on to the
punt. It was on the Wednesday, the middle of the second week
of my stay, that the police had found the body.

'I ought to have asked Miss Seldon which day it was that Bell's class found that their work on the punt was ruined,' I said.

'That hardly matters,' said Dame Beatrice, 'until we have more evidence to give the police.'

'Until we know who buried the body?'

'Yes. I think we may assume that it was not buried until after the Sunday procession. The amateur undertakers would not have taken the risk of having their efforts brought to notice too soon and by so many people, for, no doubt, all of Lower Gushbrook would have turned out to see the cavalcade of cars go by, especially as some of the cars would have been carrying the local notables.'

'So what it boils down to,' I said, 'is that somebody, somewhere, kept the corpse frozen and hidden for the better part of a week before he buried it.'

'Yes, it looks like that.'

'But who would dare to keep it hidden away so long?'

'Presumably the owner of the freezer where it was stored. It seems unlikely that anybody else would dare, and that fact must surely reduce the list of suspects.'

'It certainly seems to wipe Effie Winters's name off it. Even if she could have had access to the sheikh's outhouse, she couldn't possibly have kept the corpse in the freezer for several days without one of the kitchen staff finding it.'

'I wonder what Hallicks thinks about that?'

Guided, I suppose, by my report of my visit to the school, Hallicks went along to check it and to ask for a special interview with Mr Bell. The next move, however, did not come from him. Although Innes and I were gentlemen enough not to ask her any questions, I have always thought that Mary was the instigator of the next step which was made towards the unmasking of Winters' murderer.

She said, in that artless way which causes the experienced and prudent man to take cover and cross his fingers,

'Mike, you remember that woman reporter who came to see you when we were out that day? The one who knew it was Hamid who got caught in the man-trap?'

'What about her?'

'Would you call her intelligent?'

'As women go, yes, I suppose so.'

'Do you think she would make a good speaker?' she went on, ignoring the chauvinistic gibe.

'Most women make good speakers. Yours is an eloquent sex.'

'It's not a bit of use for you to tempt me to throw this at you,' she said, taking up a pat of butter she had just removed from her shopping-basket. 'Listen – and give up the snide allusions. I've been asked to find a speaker for the next W.I. meeting. We were to have had a flower-arrangement expert, but she's cried off, so it's up to me to find a stand-in. I've been racking my brains—'

'And out of your head sprang Minerva, as from the head of Jupiter. I see.'

'Do you think she would come? I expect we could rustle up a fee as well as her expenses, and give her a cup of tea, and at least she could get a column or two for her paper out of it. We haven't had a newspaper reporter – well, not since I've been a member – and even if this one wasn't much good as a speaker, at least she would fill in a gap. Of course, Miss Upcerne is always ready – in fact, eager – to oblige, but I'm sure we'd all prefer somebody from outside.'

The result of this conversation did not please Hallicks very much. He rang up Innes some days later and, according to what my brother told us, sounded disgruntled, not to say querulous.

'There's been a leakage,' Innes explained, 'and one of the local papers has jumped the gun. Hallicks got a clear account from Bell of the school punt project and he agrees that the body could not have been buried until much later than we thought at first. Now the papers have got hold of this – how, we don't know. The upshot is that the Women's Institute are organising a petition for Effie Winters's release on the grounds that her alibi stands firm. She couldn't have been in this neighbourhood when the burial took place.'

'How do they make that out?' I asked, glancing at Mary, who was reclining on the settee with her feet up and looking down at a book which I was pretty certain she was not reading.

'It seems there was lots of natter after the woman journalist had given her talk to the W.I. and I suppose the wretched girl put two and two together with the result that the paper came out strong in defence of Effie Winters and rather more than hinted that it was time for second thoughts about her having been arrested. Hallicks himself has been having second thoughts, too, but he isn't ready to make a move yet. He's rightly cheesed off that these women seem determined to force his hand.'

'I don't know about that,' said Mary, closing her book with what I took to be a defiant snap. 'What we think is that, if Effie Winters didn't do it, then every day she spends locked up is a blow against the most elementary human rights.'

'Which, according to the W.I., are?' I enquired.

'Not merely according to the W.I., Mike, so don't ask silly questions to which you don't need an answer. Effie Winters, as our posters will state – and we intend to have them on hustings in the Square and in every shop window on pain of losing our custom if they don't conform and display a poster – is entitled, like everybody else, to life, liberty and the pursuit of happiness.'

'You'll get me shoved off the Bench,' said Innes.

'Life, for Effie Winters, is not in jeopardy,' I said. They've done away with hanging. Happiness is a blue-bird and chasing birds is a mug's game because you can't catch up with them unless they are pulchritudinous and unfeathered. Besides, what constitutes liberty is a moot point. Think of Richard Lovelace.'

'Why should I?'

' "Stone walls do not a prison make, Nor iron bars a cage." '

She flung her book at me, and pretty accurately, too. I fielded it, returned it with a bow and remarked that I now knew the origin of the phrase.

'What phrase?' she said. 'Anyway, we've got Okeford on to the case, and if Effie isn't released when she comes in front of Innes and Lord Maumbury next time and they remand her again, Okeford is going to apply for a writ of Habeas Corpus.'

'Can he do that?' I asked Innes.

'Oh, yes,' he replied. 'To refer to Smith and Keenan's *English Law,* although I speak from memory, a writ of Habeas Corpus provides that a man or woman kept in custody without legal justification is entitled to be released. Application can be made to any judge during vacation time. There has to be an affidavit, of course, and the application must be made through counsel alleging unlawful detention. On the facts as we now have them, I'm bound to say that I think the application in Effie Winters's case would succeed. Hallicks must realise this. When Effie is brought up next time I think we shall have to let her go. One thing, so long as she is not brought to trial and acquitted, Hallicks can always pull her in again if fresh evidence turns up which is not in her favour.'

The women were as good as their word. Posters splashed out in black paint appeared like a sinister rash on boards set up in the Square and stuck in all the shop windows. Even the Stag, with or without the manager's permission, sported a double-sided board at the side of the entrance, which read: FREE EFFIE WINTERS IN THE NAME OF JUSTICE.

'I knew no good would come of having a woman Prime Minister,' said Innes. 'These girls have got it properly up the nose. The worst excesses of the Suffragette Movement are current in our midst. The *Free Effie Winters* contingent have got Hallicks exactly where they want him. It's only a matter of time before the battle-cry of the Women's Institute has us *all* by the short hairs.'

'Looking at it fairly,' I said, 'I think Hallicks was a bit premature in arresting her. He can't prove where the murder took place, he hasn't found the murder weapon and all the evidence he's got against Effie so far is that she is known to have quarrelled with her brother and that she stands to gain financially from his death. In any case, there must have been more than one person involved. Effie, so far as we know, had no means of transporting the body to Lower Gushbrook and although it might be possible for one person to have buried the body in that punt, two – and at least one of them a man and one accustomed to heavy work – would be far more likely to have done it.'

'The sheikh has some pretty hefty bodyguards, didn't you say, Mike?'

'Judging by that couple of Nubians I saw guarding his woods, hefty is the *mot juste* and they would do anything they were told, I expect.'

'I wonder whether the sheikh believes that Winters was behind Chettle and the other lad over that man-trap business?'

'Except that Winters may have been killed before the man-trap came into operation – that's a question which will never be answered satisfactorily, I imagine.'

'Oh, I don't know. It depends upon who the murderer is, don't you think? Excluding Effie, what's your guess?'

'Breedy, of course. He's a ruthless sort of chap and his son was being blackmailed.'

'And we know he's got a deep freeze.'

'Yes, but he made no secret of the fact, and, there again, so has the sheikh got a deep freeze.'

'And so have most of the big houses, I expect, and some of the other farmers. I'm sure Winters was murdered because of his blackmailing activities. Hallicks may have to cast his net a good deal wider than he thinks.'

So time passed: Effie Winters was released without the formidable aid of Habeas Corpus, Dame Beatrice returned to the Stone House and I, in spite of a pressing invitation from Mary and Innes to stay on in Strode Hillary, went back to London to get on with my book and take part in the usual round of literary meetings and functions. I also planned a fishing holiday in Scotland. Innes promised to keep me in touch with events in his part of the world, but it was not until I received a telephone call from Dame Beatrice that I realised she was far from giving up the enquiry into the circumstances of Winters's death and his extraordinary burial.

'I suppose you are too busy to come and see me,' she said, 'but if you *could* spare a few days, a room with a writing-table shall be placed at your disposal, I have a well stocked library and the New Forest is looking its best. There is garage space for your car, a horse to ride, beautiful walks at hand and,

if such matters interest you, a French chef who is a culin-
ary artist and his French wife who will do her best to spoil
you.'

Well, my novel had reached a stage where it could be left to
cook for a bit and a few days in the New Forest seemed a
delightful prospect. I accepted the invitation gratefully and it
was arranged that I should arrive in the village of Wandles
Parva in time for lunch on the following Tuesday.

A very pleasant surprise awaited me. Innes and Mary were
there, too, so the Strode Hillary party was all together again,
but this time in an environment uncomplicated by man-traps
and murder. I asked Mary jokingly whether all the W. I.
posters were down. She replied that they were, and that they
had certainly done their job.

'Martha has sold her house,' she added, 'and gone to live at
Breedy's farm, and she has got rid of the girl.'

'What girl?'

'The young girl who used to look after Breedy and call him
Gaffer.'

'Wasn't she pleased with the girl's work?'

'I have no idea. All she asked was whether I would like to
take the girl on, but I said I was quite satisfied with my Mrs
Platt. However, Miss Upcerne found the girl a very good place
at another farm, so she is quite all right.'

'Tell me,' said Dame Beatrice, 'does the girl live in?'

'She does now, because there are a wife and two children at
the new farm. She didn't at Breedy's because there was no
other woman in the house, so her mother wouldn't allow her to
stay there at night.'

'And is the Breedys' a happy marriage?'

'I have no idea, Godmother. It was a very surprising one to
most of us. One thing, though: it has taken Martha out of our
orbit. She was on our necks a bit, you know. We see nothing of
her nowadays, for which I must say Innes and I are rather
thankful.'

'Did Breedy's foot heal up all right,' I asked. 'He didn't
appear to be limping when he saw Mrs Lorne into what I
suppose was the wedding car.'

'Oh, he's as healthy as an ox,' said Innes. 'His flesh would heal up all right. I wonder what he was up to, though, to go sticking a fork through his foot?'

'Burying the body, I expect,' said Laura Gavin, Dame Beatrice's secretary. We all looked at her in what Keats has called 'a wild surmise' and it was Mary who exclaimed:

'Good heavens! So *that's* why he married Martha Lorne!'

'Hey! Steady on,' said Innes, but he looked alert and interested.

'Could be, I suppose,' I said.

'Laura often hits the right nail on the head,' said Dame Beatrice, directing at the large and comely Mrs Gavin an indulgent leer, 'and without any attempt at logic, which is so refreshing of her.'

'And, even more often, Laura hits her own thumb instead of the nail,' said Laura, with what I felt certain was false modesty. She went on, 'Anyway, if one or other or both the happy couple is or are guilty of murder, you must admit that the marriage has its useful side. Husband and wife can't be called upon to testify against one another in court, and *that's* logic, isn't it?'

'Suppose,' said Mary, 'that you had to pick one of them as the actual murderer and the other as the accessory, what would you say?'

'Oh, Breedy as the murderer,' said Innes. 'He's got the thews and sinews.'

'Women have been known to handle daggers before now,' said Laura.

'Breedy wouldn't make an accomplice of a woman,' said I. 'If one of them is guilty, it would be Martha. Breedy would merely have helped her out by burying the body for her.'

'I wouldn't have called him *that* sort of chivalrous knight errant,' said Innes. 'What do *you* say, Dame Beatrice?'

'Only that I wonder what date is on the marriage certificate,' she told him. Innes looked at her in surprise, but, before he could comment, Laura Gavin said:

'From what Dame B. has told me, I should have thought he would have married Effie Winters if he married anybody at all.'

'He couldn't. She was being held for trial when Mike saw Breedy and Martha going off together,' said Innes.

'I know that. I only meant that the other marriage would have been more likely, somehow. Still, I haven't met any of the parties concerned, so I've no business to offer suggestions,' said Laura. 'Besides, the marriage need have nothing whatever to do with the murder. *He* was a widower, she a widow. Why shouldn't they have teamed up?'

'If there had been no reason to suspect that it wasn't exactly a love-match, Martha would have told me about it,' said Mary.

'Why would she?' I asked. 'She didn't tell you anything about her husband's death and it seems to me that that was a great deal more dramatic and interesting than any mere wedding.'

I came down to breakfast on the following morning to find that Innes and Mary were breakfasting in their room, that Dame Beatrice had breakfasted and was in the garden cutting flowers for the house and that there was no sign of Laura. A young parlourmaid looked after my meal and in answer to a question told me that Mrs Gavin had gone riding and was not expected back until round about lunchtime. I said I was sorry I had missed breakfasting with her and Dame Beatrice, and asked the girl which was the pleasantest walk I could take that fine morning. She directed me, so I picked up an ashplant out of a stand in the hall and went into the garden to ask permission of my hostess to make myself scarce for an hour or two.

'For the whole day if you so desire, Mr Michael,' she said. 'Are you a great walker?'

'I think I could be, in this countryside,' I said.

'So we will not delay lunch for you, should you decide to roam the forest wild. Nothing is more frustrating than to have to cut short a walk merely for the sake of returning in time for a meal.'

'Do you know, I think I'll take you up on that, Dame Beatrice,' I said gratefully. 'I'll get some food somewhere or other, and state definitely that I won't be back to lunch.'

I said this partly for my own sake, of course, but also because I thought she and Mary and Innes might like to be together without either Laura Gavin or myself for company. I think she understood this, for she stuck an early rosebud in my buttonhole, gave my sleeve a reassuring little pat, cackled in a pleased manner and wished me a happy day.

What happened next I find difficult to account for, let alone explain. The directions the little parlourmaid had given me took me to the level-crossing at Brockenhurst just outside the railway station. A train was signalled and on some irrational impulse I charged into the station, asked where the train was bound for, took a ticket and found myself on a train which stopped at Bournemouth and then at all the stations between that resort and my destination. I got out at Ropewalk, still feeling very much surprised at myself. Then, as though all the public transport had decided to place itself at my disposal, I just managed to catch one of the few-and-far-between buses and went to Strode Hillary.

I got off the bus in the market square and went into the Stag. I thought I would have a drink and stay for lunch. What I should do with myself after lunch, before I caught a train back to Brockenhurst, I had no idea. There were two or three people in the bar, but it was too early for the usual pre-lunch crowd. I took my drink to a table at the far side of the room facing the street door, and I had hardly taken a sip when an acquaintance of mine came in.

She spotted me at once, as she could hardly fail to do, and came straight over to my table. She was the young woman reporter who had met me at Innes's house. I stood up and greeted her and asked what she would have. When I brought her gin and tonic over from the counter she had seated herself and laid her briefcase on one of the chairs. She thanked me as I put the glass down in front of her. I asked how she was.

'Panting and slavering,' she said.

'Really? I hope you're not overdoing things.'

'Somebody is,' she said. 'It will be in tomorrow's papers, so it doesn't matter telling you. I'd be obliged, though, if you'd keep it to yourself until it's public property. Oh, tell the other Mr Lockerbie, of course. He's a magistrate. He'll be discreet.'

'He isn't in Strode Hillary at the moment. We're all staying in the New Forest for a few days. What's cooking? You do seem rather steamed up. Is the W. I. on the rampage again?' I asked lightly.

'They may be sorry they ever put on that demonstration. Last night somebody clubbed Effie Winters to death with a bottle out of her own cocktail cabinet,' she said.

CHAPTER 16

ANOTHER MURDER

Effie Winters had indeed been killed in her own home, in the house she had shared with her brother. There was only one other fact my young acquaintance had been able to find out, but, knowing what I knew of Winters' own activities, the reason for what she went on to tell me was obvious. The house had been ransacked while Effie was imprisoned, but it was believed that the raider had not found what he was looking for and the police theory, so far as the reporter had been able to gather, was that Effie herself had let a visitor into the house almost as soon as she had been released from prison. Either she could not or would not give the intruder what he wanted (Winters' materials for levying blackmail I supposed) or there had been a quarrel for some other reason.

'But whoever it was must have given himself away as her brother's murderer,' said my young woman, 'and he dared not leave her alive to report the quarrel. Who on earth can he be?'

I gave my companion lunch and then she was kind enough to give me a lift back to Ropewalk, where she said she had a story to cover, and I caught the next train back to Brockenhurst. I wanted time to think over what I had been told. Besides, I had been given permission to tell Innes what had happened, although Dame Beatrice had not been mentioned because the reporter had contacted me first before Dame Beatrice's arrival in Strode Hillary. Besides, her interest in the case, so far as anybody but Hallicks and ourselves knew, was confined to the business of the man-trap.

In order to have time to arrange my thoughts, when I left the train at Brockenhurst I took my walk after all. A side road, mentioned by the parlourmaid, diverged from the level-crossing and led past the church and an abandoned manor house now falling into ruin. The road petered out, a little further on, into a footpath across a meadow and into woods.

I soon realised why the young girl had recommended this particular walk, for under and around the beeches was a carpet of bluebells, a veritable sea of them, interspersed here and there by bracken. The beech leaves were still young and of a most tender green and the male flowers with their pale yellow stamens dripped and dangled from the twigs and branches.

It was a longish walk, eight or nine miles, I suppose, and when I came out on a common it was to find a sizeable village before me. There was a choice between going back by road, a form of foot-slogging which did not commend itself to me, or returning by the way I had come.

I spotted the squat, square tower of a church and decided to take a short rest in one of the pews before walking back through the woods. I looked at my watch, made the time to be almost six o'clock and realised that if I did walk back I should be late for dinner at the Stone House. This seemed less than courteous to my hostess, so, instead of returning by the way I had come, I sat down in the church until six, left the church and made for the pub, and, having ordered a beer, arranged for private hire from the landlord to take me back to Wandles Parva.

'I've done private hire for years now, sir,' he said. 'My son does the driving. We've laid on the service ever since the breathalyser came in. Got the golf course nearby, you see, and gentlemen enjoying themselves in the club-house after their game are sometimes thankful to be drove home, some of them tending to become convivial as they tells each other black lies about doing the long water-hole in four.'

So I got back to the Stone House in respectable time, bathed and changed, and dead-heated with the sherry and cocktails at eight, for Dame Beatrice, at that time of year, dined at eight-thirty.

After dinner I took Innes aside.

'Yes,' my brother said, 'you've been bursting with news, haven't you? Let's have it.'

'I've been back to Strode Hillary,' I said.

'The devil you have!'

'Something has happened.'

'Hold it,' he said. ' "For look where Beatrice, like a lapwing, runs close by the ground to hear our conference." '

'That is not gallant, courteous, or even true,' I said, 'but I take your point. I'm pledged to give nobody but yourself my news. However, the newspapers will have been put to bed by now and the story will break tomorrow, so I feel I am quit of my oath and I think Dame Beatrice ought to be in on this. I've been told that Effie Winters has been murdered.'

'Effie Winters?' He was suitably astounded. 'But why?'

'Her house was ransacked while she was out of it, and somebody must have called again almost as soon as she got back. Whatever he had been looking for I would say he did not find. My bet is that Effie had to be liquidated so that the visitor could keep his identity secret. He must be our murderer.'

'It must be something to do with Winters' blackmailing larks.'

'Of course it must. Get Dame B. We need her to help sort this one out.'

'I suppose you didn't talk to Hallicks while you were in Strode Hillary?'

'No. I don't think my girl reporter was supposed to have blown the gaff, you see. I couldn't let her down. Besides, I don't see what good it would have done to go to Hallicks. He wouldn't have blessed me, anyway. He's probably got his hands full with two murders on his plate.'

'Not so mixed a metaphor as one might suppose at first hearing,' said Innes. 'How do we detach Dame B. from Mary and Laura without their ears beginning to flap?'

Dame Beatrice settled this little problem by coming into the room where we were and observing: 'As you are both standing on the hearthrug and the decanter appears to be untouched, matters of great moment seem to be pending. Your day, Mr Michael, must have been more fraught with incident than you either suspected or intended it should be.'

I remedied the omission with regard to the port and she took a glass with us. We seated ourselves at the table again – it had

been cleared except for the decanter and the glasses – and I
told my story.

We were not left in doubt as to our next course. That is to say,
Dame Beatrice was in no doubt about hers. In the morning she
put her proposition to us. Innes and Mary were to continue
their stay at the Stone House with Laura while Dame Beatrice
and I returned to Strode Hillary to find out more about Effie
Winters' death. I thought Laura looked disappointed at being
left behind and apparently Dame Beatrice thought so, too, for
she explained that I knew the place and the people and could
take notes in shorthand. Laura herself could do this, of course,
so it was my acquaintance with the locality which counted.

I enjoyed the drive. We went through the New Forest to
Ringwood and on to Dorchester, and then continued on the
west route past Maiden Castle and on to Ropewalk before we
turned north to Strode Hillary and the police station. Hallicks,
we were told, was continuing his investigations at the scene of
the crime.

'So we cannot intrude there,' said Dame Beatrice. 'From
what little knowledge I have of her, the person of our
acquaintance most likely to have gathered any of the known
details is your friend, the new Mrs Breedy. Will you direct
George to her house?'

'Won't she be up at Breedy's place?' I asked.

'That is what we may be able to find out,' she replied.

I was mystified by this and even more mystified by our
reception, for Martha was not only back in her own home, but
in a state of alarm and despondency. She opened the door to
us herself and appeared to be alone in the house.

'I can't talk to anybody unless my lawyer is present,' she said
in an agitated tone. 'Everything is too, too terrible.'

'Then let us invoke your lawyer,' said Dame Beatrice
briskly, 'for there is no time to lose. We tried to contact
Superintendent Hallicks, but, of course, he is hot on the trail
and one should never call off a hound which is on a hot scent.'

'You had better come in. I suppose you must have heard our
dreadful news.' Appearing a little more composed, Martha
showed us into a room which seemed to have been denuded of

most of the furniture I remembered from a previous visit with Mary and Innes. 'Yes,' said Martha, 'most of my things have been taken to the farm, of course. Do take a seat, Dame Beatrice.'

There was only one chair in the room. Dame Beatrice took it as she was directed, while Martha and I perched ourselves on the built-in window seat.

'What is known about Miss Winters's death?' Dame Beatrice enquired. 'I ask only for what, so far, is common knowledge.'

'I don't know what other knowledge you think I could possibly have,' said Martha.

'And why you feel the necessity for having your lawyer present at what is only intended as a friendly interview.'

'As to that, the village is in a state of extreme agitation. Nobody's life is safe and everybody is afraid to say much until the murderer is discovered. To think we took all that trouble to get poor Effie out of gaol and then for this to happen to her! There must be a maniac at large!'

'All murderers are maniacs,' said Dame Beatrice. 'Did any men sign the women's petition, do you know?'

'Oh, yes, quite a number. I think all our members got their husbands to sign.'

'Including yours?'

'Oh, yes, Amos and Robert both signed.'

'Robert?'

'Young Bob Breedy,' I explained.

'Oh, of course. So what is known about the death?' persisted Dame Beatrice.

'I can't talk about it. We are all afraid of reprisals.'

'Then Mr Michael and I must seek elsewhere unless, as you suggested, you are prepared to call Mr Okeford and talk in front of him.'

'I don't see how that would protect me. I am so terrified and confused that I hardly know what I'm saying. Strode Hillary used to be such a quiet, pleasant little town, but there has been nothing but trouble ever since the sheikh and his sons and those black bodyguards and the Arab servants came here.'

'Oh, you put all the disturbances down to the sheikh, do you?'

'Well, it was he who turned the indoor staff away from Bourne Farley and gave their jobs to his own people, and then there was the business of his wanting to buy Long Fallow which Breedy didn't want to sell, and then all the burglaries round and about and young Hamid Aziz getting caught in that terrible man-trap, and now two murders—'

'Of a brother and sister, so I do not see why you or anybody else need be alarmed for your own safety,' said Dame Beatrice. 'The vendetta, if such it can be called, seems to have been directed solely against Winters and his sister. 'Perhaps Mr Okeford will know why. I assume he acted for them as well as for the rest of the inhabitants of Strode Hillary. Most people need a solicitor at some time or other in their lives, be it only to buy or sell a house or make a will.'

'If you're going to see Okeford I would like to come with you. I am only here to see to the rest of my clearing-up, and there is no hurry about that. We have not yet put this house on the market,' said Martha.

'You anticipate no difficulty in selling it, I suppose?'

'Well, it is not in the best part of the town and some people might think it was damp as it's almost on our little river, but this is a very desirable part of the country with the sea so near. However, I'm afraid the murders may put people off if I try to sell too soon, so I shall not be in any hurry. I have a place to go to and I am secure financially.'

'Ah, yes, your husband's death,' said Dame Beatrice, with what I thought was a rare lack of tact. Martha, however, who seemed to be gaining in confidence all the time, merely agreed.

'Yes. His life was insured for a larger sum than I had realised,' she said. 'Excuse me. I will call up Okeford and ask for an appointment. I can hardly have him here. There is nowhere for him to sit down.' She came back after a very short interval to announce that Okeford was out of town and it was expected that he would be away for some days.

We took our leave of Martha and, as the Stag put on lunch at twelve-thirty, I took Dame Beatrice there. We spent a pleasant half-hour in the lounge, where I brought in drinks from the bar, and then we lunched in leisurely style, for the service, although adequate, was on the slow side. After lunch, to my surprise we went to Innes' house, for he had given me a key, and Dame Beatrice telephoned Okeford from there.

When she had told me at lunch that she proposed to do this, I expressed the surprise I felt.

'But it's no use, is it, if he's away?'

'It does not do to believe all you hear, although what you do not hear is sometimes useful,' she said, 'and my hearing, I am glad to say, is acute and functions well.'

'How do you mean?'

'In a house as compact as that in which we talked to the new Mrs Breedy, I should have heard the telephone. It was in the hall, only just outside the room in which we sat.'

'I didn't hear it, either, but she closed the door,' I said.

'She did not telephone Mr Okeford or anyone else. She did not intend us to visit him, I imagine.'

'But why?'

Dame Beatrice shrugged and we went out to the car. It was not far to the solicitor's house. Dame Beatrice sent in her card and we were admitted at once. Okeford greeted us pleasantly and came to the point, which he had anticipated correctly.

'The unfortunate and unforeseen death of Miss Winters, I suppose,' he said when he had seated us, 'is what brings you to me.'

'We really came to see Superintendent Hallicks. He was not available, so we made contact with Mrs Breedy.'

'Mrs—? Oh, yes, Mrs Lorne that used to be. A surprising second marriage, but I suppose the Breedys were in need of a proper housekeeper.'

It struck me that he was asking questions rather than making statements, but Dame Beatrice took his remarks at their face value.

'I think second marriages often surprise people,' she said, 'but what particularly surprised you about this one?'

'You know the details of her first husband's death, do you, Dame Beatrice?'

'I heard it was caused by a collision between his car and a lorry.'

'Breedy's lorry. She became very disorientated for a time and blamed Breedy for the accident, most unjustly, of course, but we were led to assume that she would never forgive him. That is why the marriage was such a surprise.'

'What more do you know about her?'

'Very little. I handled her affairs when her husband died and I suppose I shall be called upon again when she puts her house up for sale. What, exactly, do you want of me, Dame Beatrice?'

'I want to ask one or two questions which, with the discretion for which your profession is rightly noted, you may decide not to answer.'

Okeford smiled.

'Fire away. I'll do my best,' he said.

'Do you play golf on any day except Sunday?'

'No, except when I allow myself a vacation, and I haven't taken one this year yet.' He was too professional to appear surprised at the question, but he did ask what she was leading up to by asking it. She gave me a nod which was my cue.

'Half a minute,' I said, 'while I turn up my notes. The day before the Bounds procession was the day after Dame Beatrice came down here.' I turned back my pages. 'Ah, yes. That was the day on which Dame Beatrice interviewed the schoolboys and established that they had been responsible for rigging up the scarecrows with the smocks they had found, had added the swingle, ignored the card of buttons and had seen neither the man-trap nor the doll.'

'And that was the day on which Martha Lorne got married,' said the lawyer.

'She kept it a very close secret,' I said, adopting a light tone so as not to betray my surprise at receiving this, to me, startling piece of information. 'I thought the marriage came later. Mrs Lockerbie was doing her Saturday shopping that day and met Miss Upcerne and Mrs Sydeling. They could have known nothing of the marriage or I am sure they would have mentioned it to her.'

'Oh, I don't suppose Martha wanted Miss Upcerne and Mrs Sydeling to know all her business. They are known to be gossips,' said Okeford easily.

'But she did not go immediately to live at Breedy's farm, did she?' asked Dame Beatrice.

'Perhaps it wasn't convenient to go just then,' he replied.

'She came to see Innes and Mary on the Monday,' I said, 'and told them all about the procession. She still said nothing about her marriage, though.'

'That does seem rather strange,' said Dame Beatrice, 'since she appears to have been a regular guest at their house, whether they would or no.'

Okeford smiled again.

'She has a name for presuming upon acquaintance,' he said. 'Lonely women are something akin to hungry sharks, I fear.'

'Yes, indeed. Well, now, Mr Okeford, no more for the moment concerning Mrs Breedy, although I can see that the date of her marriage has surprised Mr Michael.'

'I gave her a lift into Ropewalk to meet Breedy,' I said, picking up my cue again. 'From the way she was attired and the Rolls Royce he had waiting for her, I'm afraid I assumed that occasion to be the wedding-day.' I was about to add details, but Dame Beatrice forestalled me.

'My next questions, Mr Okeford,' she said, 'are asked from the most disinterested motives so far as your private affairs are concerned, but answers to them would help me. They concern yourself and, more particularly, your daughter.'

This time even Okeford could not conceal his surprise.

'My daughter? She lives in Canada,' he said.

'What acquaintance had she with Robert Breedy?'

'Breedy's son Bob? I don't suppose she has ever met him except perhaps at such functions as the local flower show when she was very much younger and living here with her mother and me.'

'There was never any suggestion of an understanding between them?'

'Good heavens, no! Katie would never make a farmer's wife. Anyway, she left Strode Hillary more than three years ago.'

'You must forgive what may seem to you to have been an impertinent question. The next one may appear to be more relevant. When did Effie Winters get permission to remove her brother's personal papers from the bank?'

'How do you know about that?'

'A shot in the dark. There is no very obvious way of accounting for her death except that she had obtained the means of securing for herself a living by criminal activities.'

'I don't understand you.'

'Do you not? Winters lived largely by blackmail. I think his sister knew a good deal about his activities and intended to pursue the same line of extortion after his death.'

'But why remove the papers from the bank?' I asked.

'I think that although she knew of her brother's activities, she did not know the identity of any of his victims. She may have made some shrewd guesses, but she could not be sure until she had the evidence in her possession. It was taking a tremendous risk, since she must have realised that her brother probably was murdered simply because he was in possession of information on which he could levy blackmail, and that one of the victims had rebelled.'

'But what has my daughter to do with all this? I am most perplexed that her name has come up at all,' said Okeford.

'It came up first when I learned that Farmer Breedy claimed that his son was affianced to your daughter and that Winters was blackmailing the young man because the couple had, as my secretary would say, "jumped the gun" before the marriage ceremony could take place and, furthermore, that you yourself disapproved strongly of the match.'

I anticipated a strong reaction from the solicitor, but either his profession, or perhaps the many hazards and disappointments of the golf course, had trained him to keep his temper. All he did was to raise his eyebrows and observe that the Breedys must be mad.

'Or bad,' said Dame Beatrice. 'My inclination is to the latter supposition.'

'And that young clodhopper dared to insinuate that he had got my girl into the family way and that Winters was blackmailing him on the strength of it? Ludicrous!' burst out Okeford at last.

'So I thought at the time, although I pretended to accept Farmer Breedy's explanation. Young Breedy *was* being black-mailed by Winters, of course, but not on account of your daughter, but because the young man (and not Winters, whom the caretaker at Fell Hall accused), was the third of the local burglars.'

'How do you know that?'

'I do not know it for certain, but I was not satisfied, from what I had been told of Winters's physique and age, that the description of the man who burgled Innes Lockerbie's house tallied with Mr Michael's description of the burglar, who was presented as a young, stocky man.'

'But if it was young Breedy I met on the footbridge, he would have had to get back to Strode Hillary and burgle Innes's house before I got there,' I felt bound to point out.

'He had a car. You saw one at the farm. Moreover, you had a leisurely lunch at the inn before you returned to the house. He would have had plenty of time to get there before you.'

'Yes, now I come to think of it, there *was* a car on Breedy's gravel when the schoolboys and I crossed the farmyard,' I said. 'The only thing I can't make out, though,' I added, 'is why Martha Lorne married Breedy. She had nothing to do with the burglaries, had she?'

'No,' said Dame Beatrice. 'It was a marriage of convenience all the same as, if you remember, Laura pointed out.'

'But, if she was already married to Breedy, why her extremely festive get-up and the Rolls Royce?' I persisted. 'Anybody might have thought she was dressed for a wedding. After all, you wouldn't expect a woman – a widow - to appear in bridal veil and orange-blossom, would you?'

'And she was asking you for a lift,' said Dame Beatrice. 'One might almost suppose that she wished her attire and the Rolls Royce in Ropewalk to be noticed by somebody she knew. As for the wedding itself ... '

'I wonder whether you are both under a misapprehension about that wedding?' said Okeford.

'I think not, but I take it that you can confirm my supposition,' said Dame Beatrice. 'It was not Amos Breedy whom Martha Lorne married, but his son Robert.'

CHAPTER 17

UNWINDING A SKEIN

'How on earth did you know she had married the son?' I
asked Dame Beatrice, when we had left to return to Innes's
house so that she could write a note to leave at the
police-station for Hallicks, before we went back to the Stone
House.

'I did not know it,' she replied, 'but it was always a
possibility.'

'But whatever came over Bob Breedy? Mary told me that
Martha claims to be thirty-seven years old, but even at that I
think she is giving herself the benefit of at least eight years.
What induces a boy of twenty – the lad I caught in Innes's
house couldn't have been more – to tie himself up with a
woman in her forties? I have no wish to sound ungallant,
but, age aside, poor Martha is not exactly glamorous, is
she?'

'No. It was a marriage of convenience. The convenience in
this case is that married persons cannot be compelled to give
evidence against one another in a court of law. Laura
pin-pointed that.'

I chewed it all over and things began to fall into place. I
reviewed the various incidents which had taken place during
my stay in Strode Hillary and one thing which came vividly
back to my mind was a remark made by Innes before Dame
Beatrice appeared on the scene. I could remember word for
word what he had said, so it must have impressed me more
than I had realised at the time. I could even recall the exact
tone of his voice and the occasion on which the words had
been spoken.

'I've a feeling that, in spite of her helpfulness and general
appearance of goodwill, she's a very dangerous person. . . . I
have a suspicion that Martha Lorne is going to cause a lot of

trouble some day. . . . So far as Mary and I are concerned, there's no information to be collected. . . .' Innes had said.

Well, if Martha Lorne had been one of the murderers, as Dame Beatrice thought, she had been dangerous enough in her way, but not nearly so dangerous, I thought, as Skiddy Winters. As we walked out of Innes's house to where George was seated at the wheel of her car ready to take us back to the Stone House, Dame Beatrice said, as though she had read my thoughts (a feat I would by no means put past her):

'I don't like blackmail.' When we were in the car and were taking the left-hand bend which would bring us into the Square, she added: 'Of course, the chances are that Martha *did* tamper with the brakes of the car. Winters was able to convince her that he knew she had done so and it must have been her own guilty conscience which did the rest.'

'So you think she may be a treble murderess.'

'At any rate a double one, and it was very interesting that there was the doll, you know. I don't believe either Breedy or his son have the type of mentality to make a connection between the name Winters and a doll in the form of a snowman.'

'I hadn't thought of it, either. Boys and men haven't much affinity with dolls. There was the darning-needle, too.'

'And we do know that the doll was not stolen from the museum at the same time as the other exhibits.'

'I still can't see how Chettle smuggled out the man-trap, the swingle and those two large smocks without being spotted by the curator.'

'Oh, thereby, I think, lies the slightly slanted truth as told by Chettle. I think Hamid asked to borrow the things. The man-trap was his own idea, remember. It was after there was all the police investigation that the curator claimed that the articles had been stolen. He knew that his word would be taken against Chettle's if Hamid's life was lost. He lent the man-trap to please a very rich man's son, not dreaming any harm would come of it.'

'Still, Chettle would have been jugged, anyway, for his part in the burglaries,' I said. 'What about Batcombe?'

'I shall put in a word with Innes. Batcombe will be more

fortunate than he deserves to be. No godly, righteous and sober youth should associate with Chettle.'

'Do you think he's a psychopath?'

'Chettle? I think he is fully responsible for his actions.'

I returned to the doll. Her deductions about it intrigued me.

'Somebody could have put the connection between the doll and the surname into somebody else's head,' I suggested. 'It need have nothing to do with Martha.'

'Agreed, but I feel that both the Breedys would consider the thought too fanciful to merit serious consideration. Besides, the darning needle suggested a woman, as you thought, particularly as a thimble would have been necessary in connection with it.'

'A thimble isn't the only thing you could use to push a needle in far enough.'

'Agreed,' she said again.

'What put you on to the Breedys?'

'Oh, you had mentioned your would-be suicide to Innes and Mary, and when they told me of the incident I could not imagine a young man in these times being so much in awe of his father over a girl as I learned later that Robert Breedy was supposed to be.'

'Hamid Aziz was in awe of *his* father.'

'The two cases are not comparable. The religious and racial aspect is one thing, and the idea that Mr Okeford would demand money for allowing his daughter to marry into Breedy's family is quite another and is, to use Okeford's own word, ludicrous. Besides, the Arabs' story was genuine, the Breedys' completely false.'

'So you cast about for another explanation of Bob Breedy's urge to commit suicide?'

'Not at first, but I felt, when I heard of it, that fear of his father seemed an unlikely explanation in Bob's case. Then your recollection of the third burglar as a youth whose description would have fitted a young man of twenty—'

'Yes, I ought to have realised that, I suppose, but the caretaker told the police that his accomplice was Winters. Remember, too, that I had never met Winters.'

'Neither had I, but whereas a young actor does not find it

difficult to represent himself as being older than he is, it is a task requiring great skill and technique for an older man to appear a good deal younger than his real age. I did not believe that Winters, a man approaching middle age, could have led you to think that he was a youth.'

'What made you think that her attempt to continue her brother's blackmailing tactics led to the murder of Effie Winters?'

'The mere fact that she *was* murdered. In other words, the murderer realised that the murder of Winters had scotched the snake, not killed it.'

'What about the deep freeze?'

'My suspicions having taken the direction they did, again the Breedys appeared to be implicated.'

'Breedy made no bones about admitting that he possessed one of the things.'

'Why should he have denied it? Lots of people would have known about it and other farmers had one.'

'How does Martha Lorne come into it, apart from the doll and the darning-needle?'

'Martha Lorne Breedy is the kind of woman who, in a small town such as Strode Hillary, probably has a finger in everybody's pie. It seems that the burglary at Innes's house was the last which was carried out. There must have been a great deal of talk about the burglars' previous exploits and various theories put forward as to their identity, especially as there must have been rumours that they might be local men.'

'And my description, such as it was, of the young chap I found in Innes's kitchen could have confirmed this, you think?'

'I think it suggested something to Martha and it was then, I think, that she made contact with Robert Breedy. She herself was being blackmailed by Winters on the strength of the failure of the brakes of her husband's car and I think she may have held the whip over Robert and accused him of being one of the burglars.'

'But wasn't that a very dangerous thing to do?'

'No, because she pointed out that he and she had a common cause and that if Winters died their troubles would be over.'

'What, a Thompson and Bywaters case?'

'Oh, I think not. There was no question of a love-affair between them. Their marriage was a mistake.'

'Yes, I suppose it did rather give the game away.'

'It certainly did to Okeford, I think. At any rate, she worked upon the young man, no doubt neither of them realising, up to that point, that Effie Winters could turn out to be quite as dangerous as her brother. It was easy enough to get Winters up to Breedy's farmhouse at a time when, I imagine, Amos Breedy was at the public house and the little maidservant had finished her day's duties and gone home. Winters was still negotiating with Breedy for the sale of Long Fallow to the sheikh, you will remember, so he would not be surprised at receiving a summons purporting to come from Amos, but actually sent by Robert. A little later on, when the murder had been committed, Amos Breedy knew what had happened because the body in his deep freeze could not be hidden from him. He was guiltless of the murder, but was willing to hide the evidence of his son's crime.'

'You think young Breedy did the actual stabbing, then?'

'It seems more likely to have been a strong youth's confident blow rather than the more frenzied and probably messy attempts of a woman, although Martha, frightened by Winters's domination, must have been the moving spirit, I think. Still, a young man expert at slaughtering pigs would make a nice clean job of the stabbing of a man, no doubt.'

'What do you think they did with the murder weapon?'

'Well, we know what the weapon was in the case of Effie Winters. She was bludgeoned to death with one of her own bottles, and that, I am sure, was Martha's work.'

'Must have had fingerprints on it.'

'Yes, but none that are on record. The thieves were fingerprinted, but they did not kill Effie Winters. The prints do not tally. They will with Martha's, though.'

'So what did Bob do with the knife?'

'I think the weapon with which Winters was killed is somewhere at the bottom of the mere at Lower Gushbrook. The police are dredging for it, but it may take them a long time to find it. When they do, it will probably clinch the case against Robert Breedy. How much evidence there will be against his wife I do not know. She may be able to explain how her fingerprints came to be on the bottle in Effie Winters's house.'

'There is one thing, you know,' I said, 'and there could be plenty of witnesses to it.' I was remembering an early conversation I had had with Innes when I had asked him why he did not like Martha Lorne. 'She probably had a key to Winters's house. She had sets of keys to lots of people's homes so that she could go in at holiday times and feed their pets and so forth. She probably walked in on Effie, sloshed her and left the keys behind to get rid of them in the simplest way.'

I suppose the sentences were duly carried out. At any rate, the next time I went to Strode Hillary all was peace again. As I drove along the lanes, I saw honeysuckle and wild clematis in the hedgerows, yellow iris on the riverbanks, and when I got to the house all the roses were out in Mary's garden.